The Penguin Poets

Baudelaire

Charles-Pierre Baudelaire was born in Paris in 1821. His first
publication was *Le Salon de 1845*, and he earned renown as an
art critic and as a translator of Edgar Allan Poe. As a poet, his
fame rests on *Les Fleurs du mal*. The collection was published in
1857, and certain poems were condemned as an offence against
public morals; the book is now considered one of the
masterpieces of nineteenth-century French literature.
Baudelaire went to Brussels, where he hoped to earn money by
lecturing; but his hopes foundered, his health gave way, and he
was taken back to Paris, where he died in 1867.

Joanna Richardson was educated at St Anne's College, Oxford,
and she is a Fellow and Member of Council of the Royal
Society of Literature. Her publications include *Verlaine* (1971)
and *Enid Starkie* (1973); she has translated a selection of
Verlaine's poems for Penguin Books, and she is now working
on a critical biography of Victor Hugo.

KOMI
GREG

BUSCH Aeb
#4 Black Rone
Busett ma

Selected Poems

Baudelaire

Chosen and translated
with an introduction by
Joanna Richardson

Penguin Books

Penguin Books Ltd,
Harmondsworth, Middlesex, England
Penguin Books, 625 Madison Avenue,
New York, New York 10022, U.S.A.
Penguin Books Australia Ltd,
Ringwood, Victoria, Australia
Penguin Books Canada Ltd,
41 Steelcase Road West, Markham, Ontario, Canada
Penguin Books (N.Z.) Ltd,
182–190 Wairau Road, Auckland 10, New Zealand

First published 1975
Reprinted 1976
Copyright © Joanna Richardson, 1975

Made and printed in Great Britain by
Hazell Watson & Viney Ltd
Aylesbury, Bucks
Set in Monotype Bembo

CONTENTS

Contents

Tableaux Parisiens / Parisian Pictures

LES ÉPAVES / THE WRECKAGE

Contents

Pièces Diverses / Miscellaneous Poems

INTRODUCTION

Charles-Pierre Baudelaire was born at 13, rue Hautefeuille, in Paris, on 9 April 1821. His mother was twenty-eight, and she was the second wife of Joseph-François Baudelaire, who was sixty-two. Caroline Archimbaut-Dufays had been an orphan, without private means, at the time of her marriage in 1819; François Baudelaire, a scholar, and a man of notable integrity, had been tutor to the children of the Duc de Choiseul-Praslin. He had strong religious views, and a courtly manner which seemed to belong to the *ancien régime*. Baudelaire was to inherit his father's concern with religion, his elegance and his integrity. One may also note a less fortunate legacy, which seems to have come to him from both sides of his family. Claude-Alphonse Baudelaire, François's son by his earlier marriage, was to die in 1862 after a cerebral haemorrhage which left one side of his body paralysed. Mme Baudelaire, the poet's mother, was to end her days aphasic, like her son. There is no need to attribute the deterioration in his health – or, indeed, his final agony – to the excesses of his youth.

Baudelaire was born in comfortable circumstances, and his early years were spent in uneventful happiness. His parents loved him with devotion; his father taught him the rudiments of Latin, and tried to instil in him his own affection for the visual arts. Father and son were close to one another, and, throughout Baudelaire's unsettled life, François's portrait was always to hang at the head of his bed.

In 1827 François Baudelaire died; and, the following year, Mme Baudelaire married Colonel Aupick. It was a distinguished marriage. Aupick was superbly handsome, he had already received swift promotion, and he was friendly with the princes of the House of Orléans. He was duly promoted general commanding the Paris garrison, and later given command of the department of the Seine. He possessed the virtues of a senior army officer; presumably he also had those of a diplomat, for he was appointed ambassador in Constantinople and then in Madrid. He finally became a Senator under the Second Empire. He clearly tried to win the affection of his stepson; but he had little in common with a temperamental child, enamoured of fantasy and passionately eager for independence.

Baudelaire suffered deeply from his mother's second marriage: it seemed to him a betrayal of the love which she owed to his father and to himself. Jacques Crépet, in his biographical study of Baudelaire, maintains that he was incurably wounded.

After a few months when, no doubt, he was entrusted to Mariette – 'la servante au grand cœur' of his future poem – he began his formal education. He was sent to college in Lyons and then to the Lycée Louis-le-Grand in Paris, according to Aupick's change of garrison. He distinguished himself in Greek and Latin, but, introspective and highly strung, he suffered from the roughness of his schoolfellows. Finally he passed his *baccalauréat*; the time had come for him to choose his career. The Aupicks wanted him to be secretary at an embassy. He announced his determination to devote himself to literature.

It was hardly an ambition to earn the General's approval. He and his wife understood the value of security. Besides, at that time – in 1838 – Baudelaire had not written a line which proved his literary distinction. One cannot really blame the Aupicks for lack of understanding. Perhaps one should be grateful that they did not finally oppose Baudelaire's vocation.

He began to prepare himself for his task by intensive reading. He also served his apprenticeship to life: he came to know Balzac and other Romantic notables, and he went with prostitutes in the Latin Quarter. But his longing for experience, for originality and excitement, led him into a way of life which was sure to alarm his family. In 1841, in a drastic attempt to change his mode of existence, he was sent on a voyage to India. The captain of the ship was a family friend. Baudelaire left the ship at Mauritius; but, as Théodore de Banville, the poet, was to write, in his introduction to *Les Fleurs du mal*, one must marvel at the will of Providence. As a painter of Paris and human life, Baudelaire had to be dissatisfied for ever with commonplace landscapes. 'Now he bore in his heart the huge plants and enormous flowers, the monsters and sacred rivers, the white constellations of diamonds in the skies of light. Was he not cured in advance of insignificant fields and little lambs?'

He returned to Paris in 1842. It was now that Banville first encountered him; he was profoundly impressed by Baudelaire's noble manner, and by his beauty. 'He was slight, charming, handsome as a god, having persuasion and eloquence on his lips, and, as soon as he appeared, he enchanted the eyes of men.' He had 'great, burning, humid eyes, the eyes of an oriental sultan; his sallow complexion was tinged with pink, his narrow, delicate face had delightfully rounded features. He had a vast and genial brow, and his black and curly hair was very like Paganini's.'

Baudelaire was twenty-one, and he had come into his inheritance. He lived in the Île Saint-Louis, at the splendid seventeenth-century Hôtel Pimodan, 17, quai d'Anjou. His apartment, so Banville later remembered,

was hung with a paper patterned with enormous red and black branches
. . . There were no pictures except the complete set of Delacroix's *Hamlet*, unframed, and nailed to the wall, and a painted head, in which the same Delacroix had symbolized Grief. In front of a window from which one saw the sombre river flowing past, . . . there stood an enormous walnut table . . . Some emerald glasses, some rare and precious volumes of Latin authors or ancient poets, splendidly bound . . .; and chairs as deep as the tomb for one to sit in. That was all . . . Baudelaire lived with Hamlet, that is to say with another self; and, with the accents of a wounded swan, he sang his mysterious grief.

He was already writing the poems of *Les Fleurs du mal*.

It was almost certainly late in 1842 that he met the mulatto woman known as Jeanne Duval or Jeanne Lemer. Her real identity remains a mystery, but it is thought that she had played subsidiary rôles at the Théâtre de la Porte Saint-Antoine. She was sallow rather than dark, with remarkable, large eyes, a splendid head of hair, and majestic bearing. Baudelaire was to write in his letters that she was 'his only distraction, his only pleasure, his only friend'. He set her up, now, in an apartment in the quartier Saint-Georges. She was licentious, sly, unfaithful, illiterate, extravagant and – in time – besotted with drink. But no doubt her presence was good for him, at least in the early years; and this opinion is strengthened by the cycle of poems in *Les Fleurs du mal* which is known as the cycle of Jeanne Duval. The three or four violent poems which it contains have other sources of inspiration. The poems in which we undoubtedly recognize Jeanne Duval – among them *Le Balcon* – are the most fervent and grateful hymn of love.

And here, perhaps, one should raise the question of Baudelaire's sexual needs and abilities. One wonders if venereal disease had its effect on his virility. The poems he wrote for Jeanne Duval are passionately sensual; but they never speak of the act of love, or of the fulfilment of desire. They suggest a man who was not normally satisfied: a man whose most intense satisfaction came perhaps from visual admiration, from the exotic fragrance of his mistress's hair, from the vivid dreams which she inspired. Even in her bed, which he praises in his poetry, his pleasures seem to have been very largely those of the imagination. Nadar the photographer – a friend of Baudelaire's – said that he died a virgin. One suspects that Baudelaire was bound all the more to Jeanne Duval because she understood and accepted his limitations and his demands.

*

Baudelaire had many reasons for anxiety and distress. His journey to the East had not made him more conventional. He was still devoted to his mother, and he was still seeking to educate himself; he was also smoking hashish and opium and frequenting prostitutes. In the two years after his return from Mauritius, he spent half his inheritance. In 1844, despite his angry protests, his family arranged for a *conseil judiciaire* to administer his finances. Henceforward he was to live on a small but regular allowance; he was to be exiled from society and to move from one poor hotel room to another. The aesthete was denied a life of elegance and beauty, the independent writer was to depend on the favour of editors and readers. In all his life – so he later told Catulle Mendès – he earned only fifteen thousand, eight hundred and ninety-two francs, sixty centimes.

Such were his misery and anger at his family's behaviour that he broke with his half-brother, Alphonse, and – more predictably – with General Aupick. He attempted suicide, but failed. Finally he turned to literature. In 1845 he published his first *Salon*; it established him as one of the foremost art critics of the century. In 1846 there appeared his second *Salon*. On the cover was an announcement of *Les Lesbiennes* – the original title of *Les Fleurs du mal*. It was, it seems, in 1847 that his interest was first aroused in Edgar Allan Poe. It became one of his chief enthusiasms, and in time he was to publish five volumes of Poe's works in translation.

*

Les Fleurs du mal was to be dedicated to Théophile Gautier – the Romantic poet, and the versatile author of *Mademoiselle de Maupin* and *Giselle*. In the summer of 1843, he and Baudelaire had met for the first time. They met in the salon of Fernand Boissard, man of letters, musician, painter and art-collector – and a tenant at the

Hôtel Pimodan. Boissard's salon was to leave its mark on literary history; for here *le club des haschichins* held their meetings, and Baudelaire, Balzac and Gautier were to drift into their frenetic hashish dreams.

In this romantic setting, Gautier – like Banville – observed Baudelaire with admiration. 'His jet black hair was close cropped, and, coming to regular points on his dazzling white forehead, it covered his head like a kind of Saracen helmet. His eyes, the colour of Spanish tobacco, had a deep, intelligent look, perhaps a little too searching . . . His fine, delicate nose, slightly rounded, with quivering nostrils, seemed to scent some vague and far-off fragrance.'

Baudelaire was not the only visitor to imprint himself, that day, on Gautier's receptive inward eye. In Boissard's salon he also saw Apollonie Sabatier. She was near the window and, having cast off 'her little black lace shawl, and the most delicious little green bonnet that Lucy Hocquet or Madame Baudrand ever trimmed, she was shaking out her red-brown hair, which was still wet, because she had come from the École de Natation; and her whole person, draped in muslin, exhaled, like a naiad's, the freshness of the bathe. With glance and smile, she encouraged the verbal tourney.'

Apollonie Sabatier, *la Présidente*, was to prove so important in the life of Baudelaire that one must pause a moment to recall her. She was born in 1822, the daughter of the Vicomte Harmand d'Abancourt, Prefect of the Ardennes, and Léa-Marguerite Martin, a young sempstress. Léa was duly married to Sergeant Savatier of the 47th Infantry Regiment, who agreed to recognize the child and to give her his name. The moment that Apollonie gained her independence, she changed her name to the less plebeian Sabatier. She was a young woman of radiant beauty. She also showed promise of being a singer, and she might well have sung in opera if, at a charity concert, she had not attracted the notice of Alfred Mosselman. He was a wealthy Belgian with a taste for music and Romantic painting. He installed her in the rue Frochot – in the *quartier* of the kept woman. He determined her future.

Jean-Baptiste Clésinger, the sculptor – the son-in-law of George Sand – made a bust of Apollonie, and a cast of her body. The marble statue based on the cast was the sensation of the Salon of 1847. Meissonier was to paint Apollonie at least eight times. Gautier addressed to her his famous permissive *Lettre à la Présidente*, and two poems in *Émaux et Camées*. But while Gautier proudly celebrated her physical attraction, her sculptural beauty, Baudelaire worshipped her in secret. He had met her first, it seems, at the Hôtel Pimodan; be became a fairly frequent visitor at the rue Frochot. Her abundant gaiety, her vitality and her radiant health sometimes made him bitter, in his jealous and resentful moods; but he was enthralled by the goodness of her nature. With Jeanne Duval, *la Vénus noire*, he had known the torments and complexities – and possibly the pleasures – of physical love; but Apollonie was his *Vénus blanche*. She was more: she was his Muse and his Madonna. She was an inaccessible woman: cut off from him by Mosselman, by her health and happiness, by the fact that she did not need him. She remained an unattainable ideal, a permanent, benign inspiration.

In 1852 he sent her the first of the cycle of poems he wrote for her. He sent them to her with anonymous letters, written in a carefully disguised hand. The convention of secrecy made expression easier; perhaps, indeed, it made expression possible. But the convention was always empty. The poems clearly came from an intimate of the rue Frochot; and, among her circle, only Baudelaire, profound and reticent, could have written them. However, it was only in 1857, when *Les Fleurs du mal* was published, that Baudelaire discarded his transparent anonymity. On 18 August he sent *la Présidente* his book, and with it he sent his explanation.

For the first time in her life, Apollonie Sabatier found herself loved by a man who demanded nothing in return. She had inspired devotion of a new order. And, knowing that Baudelaire was timid, wanting to show her gratitude, she did what to her was most natural, and offered herself to him.

It has been said that, for a night, she became his mistress. We shall never know if he was her lover, or if he could not bear the shame of admitting his disability. Perhaps he felt guilty at sleeping with the mistress of Mosselman, or afraid of a new and powerful passion. Perhaps *la Vénus blanche* proved to be unattractive, after *la Vénus noire*. She herself seems to have felt it, for on his drawing of Jeanne Duval she scribbled angrily: '*Son idéal!*' Whatever the reason for the disaster, his essential dream was destroyed.

'You see, my dear, my beauty', he wrote,

that I have hateful prejudices about women. In fact, *I have no faith*; you have a fine soul, but, when all is said, it is the soul of a woman. Look how our situation has utterly changed in a matter of days. In the first place, we are both afraid of hurting a good man who has the happiness of still loving you. And then we are both afraid of our own passion, because we know – at least I do – that there are bonds which are difficult to break. And then, and then . . . a few days ago you were a deity, which is so convenient, so noble, so inviolable. And now there you are, a woman. And suppose if, by some misfortune, I should acquire the right to be jealous! Oh, what a torture even to think of it! But with someone like you, whose eyes are full of smiles and favours for everyone, it would be martyrdom . . . I am rather fatalist; but I do know that I have a horror of passion – because I have experienced it, with all its degradation . . .

Most women would have been too hurt or too indignant to trouble any further about the relationship. It is a measure of Mme Sabatier's character that she used all her tact and all her understanding to play the part which she would not have chosen. She determined to be accepted as a friend.

In the meantime, in April 1857, General Aupick had died, and Baudelaire was free to transfer his idealism to his mother. Once again he had found a woman whom he could love from a distance: a woman who embodied, for him, goodness and purity of love. His need was satisfied. He had abandoned the rue Frochot; he gradually resumed the habit of dining there, and his relationship with Apollonie became solid, tranquil and affectionate.

*

Les Fleurs du mal was put on sale on 25 June 1857. Flaubert – who had recently been prosecuted for offending public morals in *Madame Bovary* – was among the first to send his appreciation. A few days later, on 16 July, *Les Fleurs du mal* was seized by the authorities; and on 20 August Baudelaire, in turn, appeared before a police court, charged with offences against public morality. He was found guilty and fined 300 francs. 'You have just received one of the rare decorations which the present régime can grant,' Victor Hugo wrote to him. 'What it calls its justice has condemned you in the name of what it calls its morality; that is another crown. Poet, I grasp your hand.'

Baudelaire's fine was eventually reduced to fifty francs. The sentence won him sympathy and publicity. But the prosecution had hurt his pride. Six of the poems were banned, and the book could not be sold until they were removed. They were omitted from the second edition in 1861 – though they were included in *Les Épaves*, published in Belgium five years afterwards. By 1864 Baudelaire's resources were exhausted, and he went to Brussels; he hoped to make some money by lecturing. His hopes foundered pitifully. He lived on in squalor in Brussels for two years, and then his constitution gave way. On 30 March 1866, he was struck by hemiplegy – or general paralysis – with aphasia and softening of the brain. He spent a few more months in Brussels, in a clinic, and then in his hotel, and at last, on 2 July, he was taken back to a nursing-home in Paris. Banville, who had seen him in his splendour at twenty-one, 'saw him die, poor, and already old at forty-six, his bald head covered with a few sparse white locks, struck by the most cruel malady which can oppress a poet. For that terrible affliction known as aphasia deprives us of the feeling of all form, and therefore of the memory of words.' On 31 August 1867 he was finally set free. Beside his tomb in the Cimetière Montparnasse, Banville spoke, for the first time, with the voice of posterity: 'The author of *Les Fleurs du mal* is not a poet of talent. He is a poet of genius.'

*

When, in 1857, *Les Fleurs du mal* was published, the effect, said Banville, 'was immense, prodigious, unexpected, a mixture of admiration and of some indefinable anxious fear'. The Parisians were accustomed to having Gavarni, Daumier and Balzac telling them the truth about themselves; but Balzac did so under the veil of fiction, and Daumier and Gavarni hid their criticism in irony and apparent fiction. Now, without any pretence at disguise, a poet of incontestable power was dragging them into the light of day. Baudelaire showed no anger, he even showed compassion, but he held out an implacable mirror to them. He had discarded his predecessors' criterion of idealized beauty. His book was honest, melancholy and as true as life itself.

In his preface, Baudelaire declares his moral and his social position. He regretfully acknowledges man's persistence in sin, and he attributes the responsibility to the Devil. But though sin exists, and though there is Spleen, there still remains the Ideal, the aspiration towards infinity. In Baudelaire's eyes, it was an essential characteristic of Romanticism. In *Bénédiction* he transforms the Romantic theme of the curse which lies upon the poet. He gives the theme a new and spiritual significance. It is – so he insists – the poet's suffering in this world which will save him in the world to come – for he has glorified suffering as a means of redemption.

The next five poems in *Les Fleurs du mal* – the complete book, not the present selection – develop the same theme: the privilege of the poet. Among these poems is the sonnet *Correspondances*. It is clear that the perception and use of these correspondences are reserved for the poet alone. This poem is mystic rather than aesthetic. Synesthesia, or the correspondence of sensations, appears here as a consequence of universal analogy, an idea which, as we know, was familiar to Baudelaire. The principle of universal analogy was Platonic in origin. There had been a revival of interest in it in the eighteenth century and, in the nineteenth century, it was fashionable currency. As early as 1832, Balzac had discussed correspondences in *Louis Lambert*. Gautier was one of the first to use them frequently in prose, and he began to do so at least as early as 1836, as a regular critic in *La Presse*. One suspects that Baudelaire owed as much to Gautier, his 'dear master', as he did to Swedenborg, the Swedish philosopher of the eighteenth century who had claimed to establish a close correspondence between the spiritual and terrestrial worlds. But, whatever the origin of his beliefs, *Correspondances* reflects a fundamental aspect of Baudelaire's work.

The first six poems of *Les Fleurs du mal* are followed by a series which express the poet's afflictions. *La Beauté* begins a purely aesthetic cycle, which ends with the *Hymne à la Beauté*: a significant poem which links aesthetics with human destiny. For Baudelaire, the ambivalence of Beauty is not simply a poetic theme. Just as man turns to Good and Evil, so art draws its resources from Satan as well as from God. That is an original aesthetic creed. At this point – with *Les Bijoux* in the first edition, and with *Parfum exotique* in the second – there begins the cycle known as the cycle of Jeanne Duval – the cycle of carnal love. Once again the satanic element is emphasized. Baudelaire introduces an essentially modern form of sensibility: it will quicken only to a beauty that contains the elements of corruption.

There follows the cycle of Mme Sabatier – the cycle of spiritual love. It begins with the sonnet 'Que diras-tu ce soir . . .' It is hard to believe that Baudelaire could have had illusions about a beautiful woman whose 'spiritual flesh' knew all the weaknesses of matter. It is probable that he simply fixed upon her the dreams of a perfect love – a love that escaped the curse of sin.

A diptych of love: perhaps one should call it a triptych, completed by the cycle of Marie Daubrun. But we cannot be sure. This cycle – which includes *L'Invitation au voyage* – does not reflect a type of love, like the others: it only reflects a kind of Baudelairean love which is less general in its significance. We know very little about the subject. The only relevant document we possess is a single letter of Baudelaire's, and this mentions merely the Christian name of the recipient. This Marie was very probably the actress Marie Daubrun, but we cannot be positive about it. Her relationship with Baudelaire is also a matter of conjecture, but it seems that the episode occurred before the episode with Mme Sabatier. The mysterious letter tells us that the actress had rejected Baudelaire's advances, and that henceforth he vowed her a devotion very like the devotion which *la Vénus blanche* was soon to inspire. And yet the poems are different in tone. Though they express paternal or fraternal affection, they are still tinged with sensuality. This is the cycle of equivocal love, and we cannot even say that all the poems were meant for the same woman. We can only say that they express similar emotions.

Tableaux parisiens form the second part of *Les Fleurs du mal*. Baudelaire was a poet of the metropolis, but his pictures are not those of a mere observer. It is still the human drama which he rediscovers in the streets. *Le Vin* is a kind of extension of *Tableaux parisiens*. Baudelaire sets drunkenness among man's unhappy attempts to escape his condition. The next section of poems, *Fleurs du mal*, again condemns temptation and the effects of pleasure.

Révolte is a manifesto of Evil and the satanic spirit. Baudelaire analyses himself, and he is haunted by a sense of damnation which moves him to revolt and blasphemy. But these cannot prevail against God, and – in *Révolte* and in *La Mort* – he longs for death and for the discovery of the Beyond. The last poem in the collection – *Le Voyage* – resumes all the themes of *Les Fleurs du mal*, and it makes their significance clear. It does not imply indifference to salvation. It expresses the despair of man, unable to raise life to the height of his desire and of his destiny.

*

Les Fleurs du mal is, in some ways, a Romantic collection of poems. It reflects more than one Romantic theme: above all, the awareness that the poet is accursed and apart. Baudelaire shows a Romantic – indeed a Gothic – concern with death and corruption, a Romantic interest in violence, a Romantic nostalgia for the past, a Romantic longing for escape: to eternity or to exotic climes. Yet no one could mistake *Les Fleurs du mal* for a production of the 1820s or 1830s. While Baudelaire has something of Vigny's pessimism, he has a depth and power which we discover in his work alone. He is not striking a Byronic pose; he does not merely study his dejection in a mirror. He is aware of his intellectual powers, his physical desires, and, above all, of his spiritual needs. He is an adult, an analyst, a man both ruthless and compassionate; he is endowed with a large capacity for pleasure and an infinite capacity for grief. He is bitter and he is vulnerable, he is aggressive and he needs divine reassurance. He is acutely aware of the flesh; but, above all, he remains a spiritual being. *Les Fleurs du mal* is the work of a Christian poet. The erotic tributes to *la Vénus noire*, the dreams of creole women and tropical horizons are superbly Baudelairean. Yet perhaps a more profound element in his nature is reflected in the last verses of *Bénédiction*, when Baudelaire considers the divine significance of the poet's suffering. And, though Apollonie Sabatier was a courtesan, she was significant to Baudelaire as a necessary spiritual figure. He did not want her as a mistress. He desired her, passionately, as a deity, a sign of redemption, the source of a spiritual renaissance. For him she was the Muse, the guide angelical. The poems he addressed to her are unique in French literature for their fusion of earthly and spiritual love.

Baudelaire wrote of love, both sacred and profane, in an accent which is all his own. He also created a new world: a world at times hermetically closed, bounded by an oppressive sky, watched by an angry God. There is no escape from it in wine, or indeed in women – except in the torrid dreams which they inspire; and there is only transient escape in recollections of childhood, or of distant and exotic travels. In *Le Voyage*, Baudelaire dismisses all the adventures of the earth, and asks to embark on death, to find something new. He has rarely known terrestrial happiness; he is the Christian pilgrim on the last stage of his progress.

The Baudelairean world is oppressive, alluring and unmistakable. It is hemmed in by seas which are cruel and angry, sultry and full of pearls. It is a world of strange and varied perfumes – how strong the sense of smell in Baudelaire! – of heady fragrances which envelop women and allure men to exotic dreams. One of the women in this world has a spiritual presence; the rest are physically seductive and, at times, inhuman. Their eyes have the glint of steel. There is a metallic quality about them. Some critics have observed a feline note in *Les Fleurs du mal*: a disturbing suavity, a sort of velvet sweetness under which we can divine the claw. It might be more true to say that woman is a bird of prey, *quærens quem devoret*. She is lethal as poison, adamant and brilliant as diamonds. Baudelaire is haunted by her unforgiving hardness and her radiance. It is an association which often recurs in his poetry.

Les Fleurs du mal may not be technically original. The only poem in which Baudelaire really seems to have invented his rhythm is *L'Invitation au voyage*. His one revolutionary innovation is in the versification, it is the complete suppression of the auditive caesura in a certain number of lines. *Les Fleurs du mal* contains needless repetitions and poor, ungainly verses; it reveals no great diversity of inspiration. But such criticisms do not lessen its final significance. Baudelaire was Romantic – if one agrees with him that Romanticism is the most recent expression of Beauty. He was the only writer of the time who owed nothing to Hugo. At times it seemed as if Hugo had marked all provinces of poetry as his own. Baudelaire solved this apparently insoluble problem by trusting to his own genius. He brought a new sensation into French poetry – and Hugo himself recognized it when he told him: 'Vous avez créé un frisson nouveau.' Baudelaire's complex décor has no counterpart in life: it comes entirely from his imagination. In this décor moves a single character, modern – and yet, by its intensity of passion, outside time. This character is the human soul, loving, and avid for delight. It is its own torturer; but it is always consoled by the poet's ineffable pity. In this book, as Banville emphasized, there is nothing false and nothing conventional. 'Life itself posed for this terrifying portrait, this grievous portrait of such imperious charm. And so Baudelaire might pass as the precursor of the realists, if he were not divided from them by an absolute and radical difference. If – as in time they were to do – he accepts all ugliness, considers every vice as his subject, . . . he never fails to ennoble them. Like Rembrandt and Delacroix he gives them the beauty which art must create, without detracting at all from the truth of its model.'

'O Lord my God!' Baudelaire had written in one of his prose poems: 'Grant me the grace of producing some fine lines which prove to me that I am not the least of men, that I am not inferior to those whom I despise.' *Les Fleurs du mal* transcends the conventionally Romantic as it transcends the merely personal. It has – in

Matthew Arnold's phrase – 'a High-seriousness' about it. It records a spiritual odyssey, it creates an original world. It is one of the supreme books in nineteenth-century French literature – indeed, in the whole history of French poetry.

In his edition of *Les Fleurs du mal* (1931), Jacques Crépet gave the poems as they had appeared in the edition of 1868, and he followed them with *Les Épaves*: the collection, published in Belgium in 1866, which included the poems banned in France in 1857. I have given the poems in the same order.

JOANNA RICHARDSON

LES FLEURS DU MAL /
THE FLOWERS OF EVIL

AU POËTE IMPECCABLE
AU PARFAIT MAGICIEN ÈS LETTRES FRANÇAISES
À MON TRÈS CHER ET TRÈS VÉNÉRÉ
MAÎTRE ET AMI
THÉOPHILE GAUTIER
AVEC LES SENTIMENTS
DE LA PLUS PROFONDE HUMILITÉ
JE DÉDIE
CES FLEURS MALADIVES

C. B.

TO THE IMPECCABLE POET
THE PERFECT MAGICIAN OF FRENCH LITERATURE
TO MY MOST DEAR AND MOST VENERATED
MASTER AND FRIEND

THÉOPHILE GAUTIER

WITH THE MOST PROFOUND HUMILITY
I DEDICATE
THESE UNHEALTHY FLOWERS

C. B.

PRÉFACE

La sottise, l'erreur, le péché, la lésine,
Occupent nos esprits et travaillent nos corps,
Et nous alimentons nos aimables remords,
Comme les mendiants nourrissent leur vermine.

Nos péchés sont têtus, nos repentirs sont lâches;
Nous nous faisons payer grassement nos aveux,
Et nous rentrons gaiement dans le chemin bourbeux,
Croyant par de vils pleurs laver toutes nos taches.

Sur l'oreiller du mal c'est Satan Trismégiste
Qui berce longuement notre esprit enchanté,
Et le riche métal de notre volonté
Est tout vaporisé par ce savant chimiste.

C'est le Diable qui tient les fils qui nous remuent!
Aux objets répugnants nous trouvons des appas;
Chaque jour vers l'Enfer nous descendons d'un pas,
Sans horreur, à travers des ténèbres qui puent.

Ainsi qu'un débauché pauvre qui baise et mange
Le sein martyrisé d'une antique catin,
Nous volons au passage un plaisir clandestin
Que nous pressons bien fort comme une vieille orange.

Serré, fourmillant, comme un million d'helminthes,
Dans nos cerveaux ribote un peuple de Démons,
Et, quand nous respirons, la Mort dans nos poumons
Descend, fleuve invisible, avec de sourdes plaintes.

Si le viol, le poison, le poignard, l'incendie,
N'ont pas encor brodé de leurs plaisants dessins
Le canevas banal de nos piteux destins,
C'est que notre âme, hélas! n'est pas assez hardie.

PREFACE

Folly and error, sin and avarice
Work on our bodies, occupy our thoughts,
And we ourselves sustain our sweet regrets
As mendicants nourish their worms and lice.

Our wrongs are stubborn, our repentance base;
We lavishly pay for confessions,
And to the muddy path gaily return,
Thinking that vile tears will our sins erase.

On evil's pillow Satan Trismegist
Our ravished senses at his leisure lulls,
And all the precious metal of our wills
Is vaporized by this arch-scientist.

The Devil holds our strings in puppetry!
In objects vile we find attraction;
Each day we sink nearer perdition,
Unhorrified, through rank obscurity.

As some poor libertine will bite and kiss
The bruised breast of an ancient courtesan,
We catch a passing pleasure clandestine,
Like an old orange squeeze out all its juice.

And, like a million helminths swarming, dense,
A world of Demons tipple in our brains,
And, when we breathe, Death in our lungs remains,
River invisible, with dull complaints.

If rape and dagger, fire and hellebore
Have not yet prinked out with designs ornate
The common canvas of our wretched fate,
It is, alas, that our faint soul demurs.

Mais parmi les chacals, les panthères, les lices,
Les singes, les scorpions, les vautours, les serpents,
Les monstres glapissants, hurlants, grognants, rampants,
Dans la ménagerie infâme de nos vices,

Il en est un plus laid, plus méchant, plus immonde!
Quoiqu'il ne pousse ni grands gestes ni grands cris,
Il ferait volontiers de la terre un débris
Et dans un bâillement avalerait le monde;

C'est l'Ennui! – l'œil chargé d'un pleur involontaire,
Il rêve d'échafauds en fumant son houka.
Tu le connais, lecteur, ce monstre délicat,
– Hypocrite lecteur, – mon semblable, – mon frère!

And yet among the jackals, panthers, hounds,
The monkeys, serpents, vultures, scorpions,
The beasts which howl and growl and crawl and scream
And in our heinous zoo of sins abound,

There's one more hideous, evil, obscene!
Though it makes no great gesture, no great cry,
It would lay waste the earth quite willingly,
And in a yawn engulf creation.

Boredom! Its eyes with tears unwilling shine,
It dreams of scaffolds, smoking its cheroot.
Reader, you know this monster delicate,
– Double-faced reader, – kinsman, – brother mine!

Spleen et Idéal / Spleen and Ideal

Bénédiction

Lorsque, par un décret des puissances suprêmes,
Le Poëte apparaît en ce monde ennuyé,
Sa mère épouvantée et pleine de blasphèmes
Crispe ses poings vers Dieu, qui la prend en pitié:

– «Ah! que n'ai-je mis bas tout un nœud de vipères,
Plutôt que de nourrir cette dérision!
Maudite soit la nuit aux plaisirs éphémères
Où mon ventre a conçu mon expiation!

«Puisque tu m'as choisie entre toutes les femmes
Pour être le dégoût de mon triste mari,
Et que je ne puis pas rejeter dans les flammes,
Comme un billet d'amour, ce monstre rabougri,

«Je ferai rejaillir ta haine qui m'accable
Sur l'instrument maudit de tes méchancetés,
Et je tordrai si bien cet arbre misérable,
Qu'il ne pourra pousser ses boutons empestés!»

Elle ravale ainsi l'écume de sa haine,
Et, ne comprenant pas les desseins éternels,
Elle-même prépare au fond de la Géhenne
Les bûchers consacrés aux crimes maternels.

Pourtant, sous la tutelle invisible d'un Ange,
L'Enfant déshérité s'enivre de soleil,
Et dans tout ce qu'il boit et dans tout ce qu'il mange
Retrouve l'ambroisie et le nectar vermeil.

Il joue avec le vent, cause avec le nuage,
Et s'enivre en chantant du chemin de la croix;
Et l'Esprit qui le suit dans son pèlerinage
Pleure de le voir gai comme un oiseau des bois.

Benediction

When, at the bidding of the powers supreme,
The Poet in this weary world appears,
His mother, terrified, aghast, blasphemes,
Clenches her fist at God, who soothes her tears.

'Why did I not breed viper's progeny,
Rather than foster this derision?
Accursed the night of pleasure transitory
When I conceived my expiation!

Since of all women you have chosen me
To be my wretched husband's hate and shame,
Since I can not this swart monstrosity,
Like some love-letter, cast into the flames,

Then I shall turn thy overwhelming hate
Upon the cursed sign of thy cruelty,
This miserable tree I'll so contort
That its infected shoots no man shall see!'

She swallows thus the foam of her despair,
And, ignorant of heavenly designs,
In deep Gehenna she herself prepares
The pyres devoted to maternal crimes.

Yet, sheltered by an Angel's wings unseen,
The Child disowned grows merry with the sun;
In all his food, in all his rosy wine,
He finds the nectar of Elysium.

He frolics with the wind, talks to the cloud,
And, lyrical, sings of the Holy Cross;
The Spirit which upon the pilgrim broods
Sheds tears to see his carefree happiness.

Tous ceux qu'il veut aimer l'observent avec crainte,
Ou bien, s'enhardissant de sa tranquillité,
Cherchent à qui saura lui tirer une plainte,
Et font sur lui l'essai de leur férocité.

Dans le pain et le vin destinés à sa bouche
Ils mêlent de la cendre avec d'impurs crachats;
Avec hypocrisie ils jettent ce qu'il touche,
Et s'accusent d'avoir mis leurs pieds dans ses pas.

Sa femme va criant sur les places publiques:
«Puisqu'il me trouve assez belle pour m'adorer,
Je ferai le métier des idoles antiques,
Et comme elles je veux me faire redorer;

«Et je me soûlerai de nard, d'encens, de myrrhe,
De génuflexions, de viandes et de vins,
Pour savoir si je puis dans un cœur qui m'admire
Usurper en riant les hommages divins!

«Et, quand je m'ennuierai de ces farces impies,
Je poserai sur lui ma frêle et forte main;
Et mes ongles, pareils aux ongles des harpies,
Sauront jusqu'à son cœur se frayer un chemin.

«Comme un tout jeune oiseau qui tremble et qui palpite,
J'arracherai ce cœur tout rouge de son sein,
Et, pour rassasier ma bête favorite,
Je le lui jetterai par terre avec dédain!»

Vers le Ciel, où son œil voit un trône splendide,
Le Poëte serein lève ses bras pieux,
Et les vastes éclairs de son esprit lucide
Lui dérobent l'aspect des peuples furieux:

All those he wants to love watch him with fear,
Or else, made bold by his serenity,
See who can hurt him and arouse his tears,
Try out on him all their ferocity.

In bread and wine which he is meant to taste
They mingle ashes and their spittle foul,
And all he touches cast aside, debased,
Declare that knowing him was criminal.

His wife goes crying in the crowded street:
'Since he finds beauty in me to adore,
I'll play the part of idol obsolete,
Like them, I'll have myself gilded once more.

I'll glut myself with incense, myrrh and nard,
With genuflexions, with meat and wine:
Discover if, in an admiring heart,
I can usurp the privilege divine!

And when I weary of this heathen farce,
My hands both strong and weak on him I'll lay.
My nails, the nails of the extortioners,
Will to his very heart cut out their way.

And like a new-fledged bird, all quivering,
I'll tear away his red heart from his breast,
And cast it to my dog, an offering
To satisfy the beast that I love best!'

To Heaven, where he sees a splendid throne,
The tranquil Poet gazes piously;
His soul, bright as a constellation,
Conceals the sight of man's hostility.

– «Soyez béni, mon Dieu, qui donnez la souffrance
Comme un divin remède à nos impuretés
Et comme la meilleure et la plus pure essence
Qui prépare les forts aux saintes voluptés!

«Je sais que vous gardez une place au Poëte
Dans les rangs bienheureux des saintes Légions,
Et que vous l'invitez à l'éternelle fête
Des Trônes, des Vertus, des Dominations.

«Je sais que la douleur est la noblesse unique
Où ne mordront jamais la terre et les enfers,
Et qu'il faut pour tresser ma couronne mystique
Imposer tous les temps et tous les univers.

«Mais les bijoux perdus de l'antique Palmyre,
Les métaux inconnus, les perles de la mer,
Par votre main montés, ne pourraient pas suffire
À ce beau diadème éblouissant et clair;

«Car il ne sera fait que de pure lumière,
Puisée au foyer saint des rayons primitifs,
Et dont les yeux mortels, dans leur splendeur entière,
Ne sont que des miroirs obscurcis et plaintifs!»

'Blessed be Thou, my God, Who givest pain
As cure divine for our impurities,
And as the very essence superfine
Which makes us strong for Thy felicities!

I know that You still keep the Poet's place
In the blest rank of sacred Legions,
That You ask him to feast in Paradise
With Thrones and Virtues and Dominions.

I know that grief's the one nobility
That earth and even hell will not withstand,
That if my mystic crown I justify,
All ages and all worlds I must command.

But the lost jewels of Palmyra old,
The unknown metals, pearls deep in the sea,
By Your hand mounted, still would not, all told,
Give this fine diadem its brilliancy.

For it will be made of pure light alone,
Drawn from the sacred source of every light,
And mortal eyes as radiant as noon
Are mournful mirrors of its splendour bright!'

L'Albatros

Souvent, pour s'amuser, les hommes d'équipage
Prennent des albatros, vastes oiseaux des mers,
Qui suivent, indolents compagnons de voyage,
Le navire glissant sur les gouffres amers.

À peine les ont-ils déposés sur les planches,
Que ces rois de l'azur, maladroits et honteux,
Laissent piteusement leurs grandes ailes blanches
Comme des avirons traîner à côté d'eux.

Ce voyageur ailé, comme il est gauche et veule!
Lui, naguère si beau, qu'il est comique et laid!
L'un agace son bec avec un brûle-gueule,
L'autre mime, en boitant, l'infirme qui volait!

Le Poëte est semblable au prince des nuées
Qui hante la tempête et se rit de l'archer;
Exilé sur le sol au milieu des huées,
Ses ailes de géant l'empêchent de marcher.

The Albatross

Often the idle mariners at sea
Catch albatrosses, vast birds of the deep,
Companions which follow lazily
Across the bitter gulfs the gliding ship.

They're scarcely set on deck, these heavenly kings,
Before, clumsy, abashed, and full of shame,
They piteously let their great white wings
Beside them drag, oar-like, and halt and lame.

See this winged traveller, so awkward, weak!
He was so fine: how droll and ugly now!
One sailor sticks a cutty in his beak,
Another limps to mock the bird that flew!

The Poet's like the monarch of the clouds
Who haunts the tempest, scorns the bows and slings;
Exiled on earth amid the shouting crowds,
He cannot walk, for he has giant's wings.

Élévation

Au-dessus des étangs, au-dessus des vallées,
Des montagnes, des bois, des nuages, des mers,
Par delà le soleil, par delà les éthers,
Par delà les confins des sphères étoilées,

Mon esprit, tu te meus avec agilité,
Et, comme un bon nageur qui se pâme dans l'onde,
Tu sillonnes gaîment l'immensité profonde
Avec une indicible et mâle volupté.

Envole-toi bien loin de ces miasmes morbides;
Va te purifier dans l'air supérieur,
Et bois, comme une pure et divine liqueur,
Le feu clair qui remplit les espaces limpides.

Derrière les ennuis et les vastes chagrins
Qui chargent de leur poids l'existence brumeuse,
Heureux celui qui peut d'une aile vigoureuse
S'élancer vers les champs lumineux et sereins!

Celui dont les pensers, comme des alouettes,
Vers les cieux le matin prennent un libre essor,
– Qui plane sur la vie, et comprend sans effort
Le langage des fleurs et des choses muettes!

Elevation

Above the lake, above the vale,
The forest, cloud and precipice,
Beyond the sun, beyond the skies,
Beyond the spheres celestial,

My agile soul, you take your flight;
And, swimmer ravished by the sea,
Flash gaily through immensity
With marvellous, virile delight.

Fly far from these miasms foul;
Go, cleanse yourself in higher air,
And drink, wine heavenly and pure,
The light unending, sideral.

Beyond the griefs and endless woes
That weigh upon our cloudy years,
Happy the spirit strong that soars
To fields serene and luminous!

The one whose thoughts, like larks, take wing
Towards the boundless morning skies,
– Who, far below, can recognize
The speech of flowers and dumb things!

Correspondances

La Nature est un temple où de vivants piliers
Laissent parfois sortir de confuses paroles;
L'homme y passe à travers des forêts de symboles
Qui l'observent avec des regards familiers.

Comme de longs échos qui de loin se confondent
Dans une ténébreuse et profonde unité,
Vaste comme la nuit et comme la clarté,
Les parfums, les couleurs et les sons se répondent.

Il est des parfums frais comme des chairs d'enfants,
Doux comme les hautbois, verts comme les prairies,
– Et d'autres, corrompus, riches et triomphants,

Ayant l'expansion des choses infinies,
Comme l'ambre, le musc, le benjoin et l'encens,
Qui chantent les transports de l'esprit et des sens.

Correspondences

Nature's a temple where the pilasters
Speak sometimes in their mystic languages;
Man reaches it through symbols dense as trees,
That watch him with a gaze familiar.

As far-off echoes from a distance sound
In unity profound and recondite,
Boundless as night itself and as the light,
Sounds, fragrances and colours correspond.

Some perfumes are, like children, innocent,
As sweet as oboes, green as meadow sward,
– And others, complex, rich and jubilant,

The vastness of infinity afford,
Like musk and amber, incense, bergamot,
Which sing the senses' and the soul's delight.

La Muse malade

Ma pauvre muse, hélas! qu'as-tu donc ce matin?
Tes yeux creux sont peuplés de visions nocturnes,
Et je vois tour à tour réfléchis sur ton teint
La folie et l'horreur, froides et taciturnes.

Le succube verdâtre et le rose lutin
T'ont-ils versé la peur et l'amour de leurs urnes?
Le cauchemar, d'un poing despotique et mutin,
T'a-t-il noyée au fond d'un fabuleux Minturnes?

Je voudrais qu'exhalant l'odeur de la santé
Ton sein de pensers forts fût toujours fréquenté,
Et que ton sang chrétien coulât à flots rythmiques,

Comme les sons nombreux des syllabes antiques,
Où règnent tour à tour le père des chansons,
Phœbus, et le grand Pan, le seigneur des moissons.

The Ailing Muse

Alas, poor muse, what troubles you today?
Your hollow eyes still hold night's visions,
And in your cheeks reflected I can see
Madness and horror, cold and taciturn.

Have the green succubus, pink Lorelei
Poured you out fear and passion from their urns?
Did nightmare, despot mutinous, waylay
And drown you in Minturnæ, Latium?

I wish your breast, exhaling health robust,
Were always filled with thoughts both strong and just,
And that your Christian blood flowed rhythmical

Like countless sounds in language classical,
Where Phœbus, father of all song, doth reign,
And Pan, great Pan, of harvests sovereign.

L'Ennemi

Ma jeunesse ne fut qu'un ténébreux orage,
Traversé çà et là par de brillants soleils;
Le tonnerre et la pluie ont fait un tel ravage,
Qu'il reste en mon jardin bien peu de fruits vermeils.

Voilà que j'ai touché l'automne des idées,
Et qu'il faut employer la pelle et les râteaux
Pour rassembler à neuf les terres inondées,
Où l'on creuse des trous grands comme des tombeaux.

Et qui sait si les fleurs nouvelles que je rêve
Trouveront dans ce sol lavé comme une grève
Le mystique aliment qui ferait leur vigueur?

– Ô douleur! ô douleur! Le Temps mange la vie,
Et l'obscur Ennemi qui nous ronge le cœur
Du sang que nous perdons croît et se fortifie!

The Enemy

My youth was nothing but a sombre storm,
Shot through from time to time by brilliant sun;
Thunder and rain such havoc did perform
That there remain few fruits vermilion.

Now I have reached the autumn of my mind,
I must with spade and rake turn gardener,
Restore again the inundated ground,
Where water hollows holes like sepulchres.

And who knows if my reverie's new flowers
Will in this soil washed like a sandy shore
Find mystic aliment to make them bloom?

– O sorrow, sorrow! Time eats life away,
The Foe obscure which does our hearts consume
Grows stronger from our blood and our decay!

La Vie antérieure

J'ai longtemps habité sous de vastes portiques
Que les soleils marins teignaient de mille feux,
Et que leurs grands piliers, droits et majestueux,
Rendaient pareils, le soir, aux grottes basaltiques.

Les houles, en roulant les images des cieux,
Mêlaient d'une façon solennelle et mystique
Les tout-puissants accords de leur riche musique
Aux couleurs du couchant reflété par mes yeux.

C'est là que j'ai vécu dans les voluptés calmes,
Au milieu de l'azur, des vagues, des splendeurs
Et des esclaves nus, tout imprégnés d'odeurs,

Qui me rafraîchissaient le front avec des palmes,
Et dont l'unique soin était d'approfondir
Le secret douloureux qui me faisait languir.

Past Life

I have long lived beneath vast colonnades
Dyed by the suns marine with myriad lights;
Their mighty pillars, splendid and erect,
Basaltic grottoes every night displayed.

The waves rolled heaven's likeness infinite,
And merged in solemn, mystic serenade
The rich and mighty harmonies they made
With all the sunset colours in my sight.

And there it was I lived in pleasures calm,
Amid the splendours, heaven and the waves,
And perfume-saturated, naked slaves,

Who gently soothed my brow with fronds of palm,
And whose unique concern was fathoming
The secret grief which left me languishing.

L'Homme et la mer

Homme libre, toujours tu chériras la mer!
La mer est ton miroir; tu contemples ton âme
Dans le déroulement infini da sa lame,
Et ton esprit n'est pas un gouffre moins amer.

Tu te plais à plonger au sein de ton image;
Tu l'embrasses des yeux et des bras, et ton cœur
Se distrait quelquefois de sa propre rumeur
Au bruit de cette plainte indomptable et sauvage.

Vous êtes tous les deux ténébreux et discrets:
Homme, nul n'a sondé le fond de tes abîmes,
Ô mer, nul ne connaît tes richesses intimes,
Tant vous êtes jaloux de garder vos secrets!

Et cependant voilà des siècles innombrables
Que vous vous combattez sans pitié ni remord,
Tellement vous aimez le carnage et la mort,
Ô lutteurs éternels, ô frères implacables!

Man and the Sea

Free man, you will for ever love the sea!
The sea's your mirror; you observe your soul
Perpetually as its waves unroll,
Your spirit's chasm yawns as bitterly.

You like to plunge into your element,
Embrace it with your eyes and arms. Your soul
At times forgets its clamour sorrowful
In this ungovernable wild lament.

You are both of you dark and reticent;
Man, none has sounded your profound abyss,
O sea, none knows your hidden treasuries,
You keep your secrets with such firm intent!

And yet for centuries uncountable
You've fought without compassion or regret,
So much do you love violence and death,
Eternal foes, brothers implacable!

La Beauté

Je suis belle, ô mortels! comme un rêve de pierre,
Et mon sein, où chacun s'est meurtri tour à tour,
Est fait pour inspirer au poète un amour
Éternel et muet ainsi que la matière.

Je trône dans l'azur comme un sphinx incompris;
J'unis un cœur de neige à la blancheur des cygnes;
Je hais le mouvement qui déplace les lignes,
Et jamais je ne pleure et jamais je ne ris.

Les poètes, devant mes grandes attitudes,
Que j'ai l'air d'emprunter aux plus fiers monuments,
Consumeront leurs jours en d'austères études;

Car j'ai, pour fasciner ces dociles amants,
De purs miroirs qui font toutes choses plus belles:
Mes yeux, mes larges yeux aux clartés éternelles!

Beauty

I am fair, o humankind, a reverie of stone!
Upon my breast all mortal men have bruised themselves in turn,
For it is made to fire the poet's adoration
Silent as stone, lasting like stone for centuries to come.

I sit enthroned in paradise, a sphinx not understood,
A snow-cold heart uniting with the whiteness of the swan,
Abhorring any action which may displace a line;
Never with tears or smiles do I disturb my attitude.

The poets, seeing me adopt my grand, majestic stance,
Borrowed, apparently, from some heroic monument,
Will waste their days considering its true significance;

For docile lovers such as these I have my blandishments,
My mirrors pure which make all things on earth more beautiful:
My eyes, my great and wondrous eyes with light perpetual.

L'Idéal

Ce ne seront jamais ces beautés de vignettes,
Produits avariés, nés d'un siècle vaurien,
Ces pieds à brodequins, ces doigts à castagnettes,
Qui sauront satisfaire un cœur comme le mien.

Je laisse à Gavarni, poëte des chloroses,
Son troupeau gazouillant de beautés d'hôpital,
Car je ne puis trouver parmi ces pâles roses
Une fleur qui ressemble à mon rouge idéal.

Ce qu'il faut à ce cœur profond comme un abîme,
C'est vous, Lady Macbeth, âme puissante au crime,
Rêve d'Eschyle éclos au climat des autans;

Ou bien toi, grande Nuit, fille de Michel-Ange,
Qui tords paisiblement dans une pose étrange
Tes appas façonnés aux bouches des Titans!

The Ideal

It will not be those beauties in vignettes,
Spoiled products of a worthless century,
Those feet in half-boots, hands with castanets,
Which ever my own longing satisfy.

Gavarni, poet of anaemic girls,
May keep his babbling flock from hospital;
I cannot find among those roses pale
A flower which is like my red ideal.

What I need for this heart as deep as hell
Is you, Lady Macbeth, great criminal,
Vision of Æschylus of tempests born,

Or you, Night, child of Michelangelo,
Who, peaceful, in contorted pose, doth show
The beauties that a Titan would not scorn!

Hymne à la beauté

Viens-tu du ciel profond ou sors-tu de l'abîme,
Ô Beauté? ton regard, infernal et divin,
Verse confusément le bienfait et le crime,
Et l'on peut pour cela te comparer au vin.

Tu contiens dans ton œil le couchant et l'aurore;
Tu répands des parfums comme un soir orageux;
Tes baisers sont un philtre et ta bouche une amphore
Qui font le héros lâche et l'enfant courageux.

Sors-tu du gouffre noir ou descends-tu des astres?
Le Destin charmé suit tes jupons comme un chien;
Tu sèmes au hasard la joie et les désastres
Et tu gouvernes tout et ne réponds de rien.

Tu marches sur des morts, Beauté, dont tu te moques;
De tes bijoux l'Horreur n'est pas le moins charmant,
Et le Meurtre, parmi tes plus chères breloques,
Sur ton ventre orgueilleux danse amoureusement.

L'éphémère ébloui vole vers toi, chandelle,
Crépite, flambe et dit: Bénissons ce flambeau!
L'amoureux pantelant incliné sur sa belle
A l'air d'un moribond caressant son tombeau.

Que tu viennes du ciel ou de l'enfer, qu'importe,
Ô Beauté! monstre énorme, effrayant, ingénu!
Si ton œil, ton souris, ton pied, m'ouvrent la porte
D'un Infini que j'aime et n'ai jamais connu?

De Satan ou de Dieu, qu'importe? Ange ou Sirène,
Qu'importe, si tu rends, – fée aux yeux de velours,
Rythme, parfum, lueur, ô mon unique reine! –
L'univers moins hideux et les instants moins lourds?

Hymn to Beauty

Come you, o Beauty, from the sky profound
Or the abyss? Infernal and divine,
Your glance sheds sin and blessing, and confounds,
And you can be compared in this with wine.

Your eyes contain the dawn and crepuscule,
You scatter fragrance like a stormy eve,
Your mouth's an amphora, your kiss a phial
Which makes the hero shy, the infant brave.

Come you from the dark gulf or from the stars?
Fate, charmed and doglike, trails your petticoat;
You sow, at random, joy and bitterness,
You rule the world, responsible for naught.

You walk, irreverent, upon the dead;
Horror is not the gem that charms you least;
Murder, among your baubles most beloved,
Dances, enamoured, on your splendid breast.

The dazzled day-fly to your candle wings,
Crackles and burns and says: I bless this flame!
The lover to his mistress murmuring
Looks like a dying man kissing his tomb.

What matter if you come from heaven or hell,
O Beauty! Monster huge, alarming, pure!
If, with your eyes, your smile, you let me dwell
In loved Infinity unknown before?

From Satan or from God, seraph or fiend,
What matter, if – fairy with velvet eyes,
O rhythm, fragrance, light, my only queen! –
You make the world less grim, time faster fly?

Parfum exotique

Quand, les deux yeux fermés, en un soir chaud d'automne,
Je respire l'odeur de ton sein chaleureux,
Je vois se dérouler des rivages heureux
Qu'éblouissent les feux d'un soleil monotone;

Une île paresseuse où la nature donne
Des arbres singuliers et des fruits savoureux;
Des hommes dont le corps est mince et vigoureux,
Et des femmes dont l'œil par sa franchise étonne.

Guidé par ton odeur vers de charmants climats,
Je vois un port rempli de voiles et de mâts
Encor tout fatigués par la vague marine,

Pendant que le parfum des verts tamariniers,
Qui circule dans l'air et m'enfle la narine,
Se mêle dans mon âme au chant des mariniers.

Exotic Scent

When, with closed eyes, on some warm autumn night,
I breathe your bosom's sultry fragrances,
Enchanted shores unfold their promontories
Dazed by a sun monotonously bright;

Nature endows this isle inanimate
With fruits most succulent and curious trees,
And men with bodies slim and vigorous,
And women whose frank gaze bestows delight.

Led by your scent to magic littorals,
I see a harbour filled with masts and sails
Still tired from the sea surge, the ocean near,

While the aroma of green tamarinds
Dilates my nostrils, fills the atmosphere,
And mingles with the song of mariners.

La Chevelure

Ô toison, moutonnant jusque sur l'encolure!
Ô boucles! Ô parfum chargé de nonchaloir!
Extase! Pour peupler ce soir l'alcôve obscure
Des souvenirs dormant dans cette chevelure,
Je la veux agiter dans l'air comme un mouchoir!

La langoureuse Asie et la brûlante Afrique,
Tout un monde lointain, absent, presque défunt,
Vit dans tes profondeurs, forêt aromatique!
Comme d'autres esprits voguent sur la musique,
Le mien, ô mon amour! nage sur ton parfum.

J'irai là-bas où l'arbre et l'homme, pleins de sève,
Se pâment longuement sous l'ardeur des climats;
Fortes tresses, soyez la houle qui m'enlève!
Tu contiens, mer d'ébène, un éblouissant rêve
De voiles, de rameurs, de flammes et de mâts:

Un port retentissant où mon âme peut boire
À grands flots le parfum, le son et la couleur;
Où les vaisseaux, glissant dans l'or et dans la moire,
Ouvrent leurs vastes bras pour embrasser la gloire
D'un ciel pur où frémit l'éternelle chaleur.

Je plongerai ma tête amoureuse d'ivresse
Dans ce noir océan où l'autre est enfermé;
Et mon esprit subtil que le roulis caresse
Saura vous retrouver, ô féconde paresse!
Infinis bercements du loisir embaumé!

Cheveux bleus, pavillon de ténèbres tendues,
Vous me rendez l'azur du ciel immense et rond;
Sur les bords duvetés de vos mèches tordues
Je m'enivre ardemment des senteurs confondues
De l'huile de coco, du musc et du goudron.

Hair

O fleece, that to the very shoulders foams!
O locks! Aroma rich with indolence!
O bliss! Tonight, to fill the alcove dim
With memories that in it slumber on,
I want it in the air like frankincense.

Languorous Asia, Africa aglow,
A whole world distant, absent, almost gone,
Lives, aromatic forest, deep in you!
As other souls to sea on music go,
Mine, o my love! upon your scent sails on.

I'll go where trees and men are vigorous,
And in the ardent climes a long time swoon;
Strong tresses, be my current bounteous!
You hold, dark sea, a vision luminous
Of sails and oarsmen, masts and gonfalons:

A port resounding where, in draughts untold,
My soul may drink in colour, scent and sound;
Where vessels glide in silky waves and gold,
And open their vast arms the heaven to hold:
A pure sky where heat quivers without end.

I'll plunge my head in love with drunkenness
Deep in this dark sea which the other holds;
And while the tides my subtle soul caress
Find you again, o fertile idleness,
O perfumed leisure endlessly cajoled!

Blue hair, the night's outspread pavilion,
The blue of boundless heaven you restore;
Upon your downy twisted locks undone,
I seek the sweet intoxication
Of cocoa-nut oil, mingled musk and tar.

Longtemps! toujours! ma main dans ta crinière lourde
Sèmera le rubis, la perle et le saphir,
Afin qu'à mon désir tu ne sois jamais sourde!
N'es-tu pas l'oasis où je rêve, et la gourde
Où je hume à longs traits le vin du souvenir?

For long, for ever, in your heavy mane
The sapphire, ruby, pearl I'll scatter free,
So that I'll never plead to you in vain:
You my oasis, flask elysian
From which I drink long draughts of memory!

«Je t'adore à l'égal de de la voûte nocturne ...»

Je t'adore à l'égal de la voûte nocturne,
Ô vase de tristesse, ô grande taciturne,
Et t'aime d'autant plus, belle, que tu me fuis,
Et que tu me parais, ornement de mes nuits,
Plus ironiquement accumuler les lieues
Qui séparent mes bras des immensités bleues.

Je m'avance à l'attaque, et je grimpe aux assauts,
Comme après un cadavre un chœur de vermisseaux,
Et je chéris, ô bête implacable et cruelle!
Jusqu'à cette froideur par où tu m'es plus belle!

'I worship you like night's pavilion . . .'

I worship you like night's pavilion,
O vase of sadness, o great silent one,
And love you more since you escape from me,
And since you seem, my night's sublimity,
To mock me and increase the leagues that lie
Between my arms and blue immensity.

I move to the attack, besiege, assail,
Like eager worms after a funeral.
I even love, o beast implacable,
The coldness which makes you more beautiful.

«*Tu mettrais l'univers entier dans ta ruelle ...*»

Tu mettrais l'univers entier dans ta ruelle,
Femme impure! L'ennui rend ton âme cruelle.
Pour exercer tes dents à ce jeu singulier,
Il te faut chaque jour un cœur au râtelier.
Tes yeux, illuminés ainsi que des boutiques
Ou des ifs flamboyant dans les fêtes publiques,
Usent insolemment d'un pouvoir emprunté,
Sans connaître jamais la loi de leur beauté.

Machine aveugle et sourde, en cruautés féconde!
Salutaire instrument, buveur du sang du monde,
Comment n'as-tu pas honte et comment n'as-tu pas
Devant tous les miroirs vu pâlir tes appas?
La grandeur de ce mal où tu te crois savante
Ne t'a donc jamais fait reculer d'épouvante,
Quand la nature, grande en ses desseins cachés,
De toi se sert, ô femme, ô reine des péchés,
– De toi, vil animal, – pour pétrir un génie?

O fangeuse grandeur! sublime ignominie!

'*You would be all creation's concubine . . .*'

You would be all creation's concubine,
Woman impure! Boredom makes you malign.
To keep your teeth sharp for this monstrous chase,
Each day with hearts you feed your ivories.
Your eyes are lit up bright like fairground stalls
And lanterns gay at public festivals;
They insolently use a borrowed power,
And never understand their beauty's law.

Unfeeling, blind machine, of malice full!
Imbiber of the world's blood, useful tool,
How are you not ashamed, how could you fail
To see in every glass your charms grow pale?
The greatness of this harm at which you're skilled
Has never, then, made you draw back, appalled,
When nature, great in its concealed designs,
Makes use of you, o woman, queen of sins,
– Of you, vile beast, – to form a genius?

Greatness unclean! Dishonour marvellous!

Sed non satiata

Bizarre déité, brune comme les nuits,
Au parfum mélangé de musc et de havane,
Œuvre de quelque obi, le Faust de la savane,
Sorcière au flanc d'ébène, enfant des noirs minuits,

Je préfère au constance, à l'opium, au nuits,
L'élixir de ta bouche où l'amour se pavane;
Quand vers toi mes désirs partent en caravane,
Tes yeux sont la citerne où boivent mes ennuis.

Par ces deux grands yeux noirs, soupiraux de ton âme
Ô démon sans pitié! verse-moi moins de flamme;
Je ne suis pas le Styx pour t'embrasser neuf fois,

Hélas! et je ne puis, Mégère libertine,
Pour briser ton courage et te mettre aux abois,
Dans l'enfer de ton lit devenir Proserpine!

Sed non satiata

Divinity bizarre, dark as the nights,
Fragrant with frankincense and with Havana,
Work of some obi, Faust of the savanna,
Black sorceress, the child of jet midnights,

No famous wines nor opium can delight,
But your lips' elixir, love's hosanna;
My desires in caravan find manna,
A well of water, in your eyes' pure light.

Through these great dark eyes, vent-holes of your soul,
Pour forth less flame! Demon, be merciful!
No Styx am I, nine times embracing thee!

Alas! nor can I, vixen libertine,
Destroy your courage and bring you to bay,
In your bed's hell become a Proserpine!

«*Avec ses vêtements ondoyants et nacrés . . .*»

Avec ses vêtements ondoyants et nacrés,
Même quand elle marche on croirait qu'elle danse,
Comme ces longs serpents que les jongleurs sacrés
Au bout de leurs bâtons agitent en cadence.

Comme le sable morne et l'azur des déserts,
Insensibles tous deux à l'humaine souffrance,
Comme les longs réseaux de la houle des mers,
Elle se développe avec indifférence.

Ses yeux polis sont faits de minéraux charmants,
Et dans cette nature étrange et symbolique
Où l'ange inviolé se mêle au sphinx antique,

Où tout n'est qu'or, acier, lumière et diamants,
Resplendit à jamais, comme un astre inutile,
La froide majesté de la femme stérile.

'Clad in her undulating pearly dress . . .'

Clad in her undulating pearly dress,
She walks as if she danced a saraband,
Like a long serpent which a sorceress
Stirs into rhythmic measure with her wand.

Like the Sahara's gloomy sand and blue,
Unmoved by the distress of humankind,
Like the long net of ocean's ebb and flow,
She stretches out, impassible, unkind.

Her polished eyes are magic minerals,
And in her nature strange, symbolical,
Where ancient sphinx meets soul angelical,

Where all is gold and diamonds, light and steel,
Shines like a useless star, eternally,
The sterile woman's icy majesty.

De profundis clamavi

J'implore ta pitié, Toi, l'unique que j'aime,
Du fond du gouffre obscur où mon cœur est tombé.
C'est un univers morne à l'horizon plombé,
Où nagent dans la nuit l'horreur et le blasphème;

Un soleil sans chaleur plane au-dessus six mois,
Et les six autres mois la nuit couvre la terre;
C'est un pays plus nu que la terre polaire;
– Ni bêtes, ni ruisseaux, ni verdure, ni bois!

Or il n'est pas d'horreur au monde qui surpasse
La froide cruauté de ce soleil de glace
Et cette immense nuit semblable au vieux Chaos;

Je jalouse le sort des plus vils animaux
Qui peuvent se plonger dans un sommeil stupide,
Tant l'écheveau du temps lentement se dévide!

De profundis clamavi

I beg your mercy, You, all that I love,
Deep in the dim gulf where my heart now lies.
It is a world of doom with leaden skies;
Horror and blasphemy float in its night.

A cold sun hangs above for half the year,
And for the rest the darkness covers all;
It is a land more barren than the Pole;
– No animals, or streams, or forests here!

No horror in the wide world can surpass
The cold unkindness of this sun of ice
And this vast night like Chaos biblical;

I envy the most abject animal
Which in dull sleep oblivion can find,
So slowly does the skein of time unwind!

Le Vampire

Toi qui, comme un coup de couteau,
Dans mon cœur plaintif es entrée;
Toi qui, forte comme un troupeau
De démons, vins, folle et parée,

De mon esprit humilié
Faire ton lit et ton domaine;
– Infâme à qui je suis lié
Comme le forçat à la chaîne,

Comme au jeu le joueur têtu,
Comme à la bouteille l'ivrogne,
Comme aux vermines la charogne,
– Maudite, maudite sois-tu!

J'ai prié le glaive rapide
De conquérir ma liberté,
Et j'ai dit au poison perfide
De secourir ma lâcheté.

Hélas! le poison et le glaive
M'ont pris en dédain et m'ont dit:
«Tu n'es pas digne qu'on t'enlève
À ton esclavage maudit,

«Imbécile! – de son empire
Si nos efforts te délivraient,
Tes baisers ressusciteraient
Le cadavre de ton vampire!»

The Vampire

Thou who, like a dagger-thrust,
Entered my complaining soul;
Thou who, potent as a host
Of demons, came, wild, beautiful,

To make my heart cast on the ground
Into your bed and your domain;
– Wretch infamous to whom I'm bound
Like the convict to the chain,

The stubborn gambler to his dice,
The drunkard to his revelry,
The carrion to worms and lice,
– Cursed, cursed may thou be!

I implored the rapid sword
To secure my liberty,
I asked the poison I abhorred
To succour my timidity.

Alas! the poison and the sword
Only showed contempt for me:
'You deserve not the reward
Of freedom from your slavery,

Fool! – If our resolution
Saved you from its sovereignty,
You would kiss alive again
The vampire's tenement of clay!'

Remords posthume

Lorsque tu dormiras, ma belle ténébreuse,
Au fond d'un monument construit en marbre noir,
Et lorsque tu n'auras pour alcôve et manoir
Qu'un caveau pluvieux et qu'une fosse creuse;

Quand la pierre, opprimant ta poitrine peureuse
Et tes flancs qu'assouplit un charmant nonchaloir,
Empêchera ton cœur de battre et de vouloir,
Et tes pieds de courir leur course aventureuse,

Le tombeau, confident de mon rêve infini
(Car le tombeau toujours comprendra le poëte),
Durant ces longues nuits d'où le somme est banni,

Te dira: «Que vous sert, courtisane imparfaite,
De n'avoir pas connu ce que pleurent les morts?»
Et le ver rongera ta peau comme un remords.

Posthumous Regret

When you lie still, beloved dusky one,
Deep in your sombre marble monument,
When you have no abode or tenement
Except a rainy vault, a hollow tomb;

When on your timid breast there weighs the stone,
Your womb is tranquil and indifferent,
Your heart no longer beats with ravishment,
Your feet no longer on adventure run,

The grave, which knows my endless reverie
(Graves understand the poet's vision),
In those vast nights which know no lullaby,

Will ask: 'What do you gain, frail courtesan,
Because you knew not what the dead lament?'
And worms will gnaw your body, penitent.

Le Chat

Viens, mon beau chat, sur mon cœur amoureux;
    Retiens les griffes de ta patte,
Et laisse-moi plonger dans tes beaux yeux,
    Mêlés de métal et d'agate.

Lorsque mes doigts caressent à loisir
    Ta tête et ton dos élastique,
Et que ma main s'enivre du plaisir
    De palper ton corps électrique,

Je vois ma femme en esprit. Son regard,
    Comme le tien, aimable bête,
Profond et froid, coupe et fend comme un dard,

    Et, des pieds jusques à la tête,
Un air subtil, un dangereux parfum
    Nagent autour de son corps brun.

The Cat

Come, lovely cat, my heart is amorous;
  Draw in your claws for me,
And let me gaze into your splendid eyes,
  Flecked with calcedony.

When, gently, leisurely, my hands caress
  Your head, your tensile back,
And grow intoxicated with the bliss,
  The aphrodisiac,

I see my mistress in my mind. Her glance,
  Like yours, endearing beast,
Cold, searching, cuts and shivers like a lance,

  Aromas sweet invest –
A subtle air, a perilous perfume –
  Her body cinnamon.

Le Balcon

Mère des souvenirs, maîtresse des maîtresses,
Ô toi, tous mes plaisirs! ô toi, tous mes devoirs!
Tu te rappelleras la beauté des caresses,
La douceur du foyer et le charme des soirs,
Mère des souvenirs, maîtresse des maîtresses!

Les soirs illuminés par l'ardeur du charbon,
Et les soirs au balcon, voilés de vapeurs roses,
Que ton sein m'était doux! que ton cœur m'était bon!
Nous avons dit souvent d'impérissables choses
Les soirs illuminés par l'ardeur du charbon.

Que les soleils sont beaux dans les chaudes soirées!
Que l'espace est profond! Que le cœur est puissant!
En me penchant vers toi, reine des adorées,
Je croyais respirer le parfum de ton sang.
Que les soleils sont beaux dans les chaudes soirées!

La nuit s'épaississait ainsi qu'une cloison,
Et mes yeux dans le noir devinaient tes prunelles,
Et je buvais ton souffle, ô douceur! ô poison!
Et tes pieds s'endormaient dans mes mains fraternelles.
La nuit s'épaississait ainsi qu'une cloison.

Je sais l'art d'évoquer les minutes heureuses,
Et revis mon passé blotti dans tes genoux.
Car à quoi bon chercher tes beautés langoureuses
Ailleurs qu'en ton cher corps et qu'en ton cœur si doux?
Je sais l'art d'évoquer les minutes heureuses!

Ces serments, ces parfums, ces baisers infinis,
Renaîtront-ils d'un gouffre interdit à nos sondes,
Comme montent au ciel les soleils rajeunis
Après s'être lavés au fond des mers profondes?
– Ô serments! ô parfums! ô baisers infinis!

The Balcony

Mother of memories, mistress of mistresses,
All I delight in, all I venerate!
Thou wilt recall the joy of each caress,
The gentle fire, the evenings exquisite,
Mother of memories, mistress of mistresses!

The evenings lustred by the burning coal,
And on the balcony, rose-veiled in mist.
How sweet your breast to me, how kind your soul!
We said much that for all time will exist
The evenings lustred by the burning coal.

How fine the suns are on warm evenings!
How vast is space – the heart's own magnitude!
As I bent close, queen of my worshipping,
I thought I breathed the fragrance of your blood.
How fine the suns are on warm evenings!

The night grew thick, like a partition,
And in obscurity I guessed your eyes,
And drank your breath, o poison! benison!
And held your feet – a brother's courtesies.
The night grew thick like a partition.

I know how to recall felicity,
And, buried in your lap, I saw my past.
Where do your sultry grace and beauty lie
But in your body dear, heart unsurpassed?
I know how to recall felicity.

These vows, these perfumes, kisses infinite,
Will they rise up from gulfs unfathomèd,
Like suns, grown young again, rise into light
When they have cleansed themselves on the sea bed?
– O vows! O perfumes! Kisses infinite!

Le Possédé

Le soleil s'est couvert d'un crêpe. Comme lui,
Ô Lune de ma vie! emmitoufle-toi d'ombre;
Dors ou fume à ton gré; sois muette, sois sombre,
Et plonge tout entière au gouffre de l'Ennui;

Je t'aime ainsi! Pourtant, si tu veux aujourd'hui,
Comme un astre éclipsé qui sort de la pénombre,
Te pavaner aux lieux que la Folie encombre,
C'est bien! Charmant poignard, jaillis de ton étui!

Allume ta prunelle à la flamme des lustres!
Allume le désir dans les regards des rustres!
Tout de toi m'est plaisir, morbide ou pétulant;

Sois ce que tu voudras, nuit noire, rouge aurore;
Il n'est pas une fibre en tout mon corps tremblant
Qui ne crie: *Ô mon cher Belzébuth, je t'adore!*

Possessed

The sun is veiled in darkness. Like the sun,
O Moon of my existence! hide in shade;
Smoke, slumber as you will; be silent, sad,
And plunge into the gulf of tedium;

But if you wish today, beloved one,
A star eclipsed in sudden light arrayed,
To flaunt in places crowded by the Mad,
So be it! Leave your sheath, dear falchion!

Light up your eyes from flaming chandeliers!
Light up desire among the cavaliers!
To me you are all pleasure – fierce, serene;

Be what you will, red dawn, night ebony,
There's not a fibre in my body keen
That does not cry: *Satan, I worship thee!*

Un Fantôme

ii

LE PARFUM

Lecteur, as-tu quelquefois respiré
Avec ivresse et lente gourmandise
Ce grain d'encens qui remplit une église,
Ou d'un sachet le musc invétéré?

Charme profond, magique, dont nous grise
Dans le présent le passé restauré!
Ainsi l'amant sur un corps adoré
Du souvenir cueille la fleur exquise.

De ses cheveux élastiques et lourds,
Vivant sachet, encensoir, de l'alcôve,
Une senteur montait, sauvage et fauve,

Et des habits, mousseline ou velours,
Tout imprégnés de sa jeunesse pure,
Se dégageait un parfum de fourrure.

A Phantom

ii

THE PERFUME

Reader, have you breathed in, now and then,
Intoxicated, with slow gluttony,
The thurible which fills a sanctuary,
A sachet's ancient fragrance muscadine?

Charm magical, profound, with which today
The past restored delights us! Heady wine!
So does the lover on some form divine
Gather the charming flower of memory.

There rises from her tensile, heavy hair,
A living sachet, censer of the bed,
A perfume savage, turbulent and rude,

And from the clothes, muslin or velvet fair,
All instinct with her youth immaculate,
A smell of fur arises, intimate.

«Je te donne ces vers afin que si mon nom . . .»

Je te donne ces vers afin que si mon nom
Aborde heureusement aux époques lointaines,
Et fait rêver un soir les cervelles humaines,
Vaisseau favorisé par un grand aquilon,

Ta mémoire, pareille aux fables incertaines,
Fatigue le lecteur ainsi qu'un tympanon,
Et par un fraternel et mystique chaînon
Reste comme pendue à mes rimes hautaines;

Être maudit à qui, de l'abîme profond
Jusqu'au plus haut du ciel, rien, hors moi, ne répond!
– Ô toi qui, comme une ombre à la trace éphémère,

Foules d'un pied léger et d'un regard serein
Les stupides mortels qui t'ont jugée amère,
Statue aux yeux de jais, grand ange au front d'airain!

' *These lines I give thee so that if mankind . . .* '

These lines I give thee so that if mankind
Recall me, happily, in years to come,
And muse, some distant evening, on my name,
A vessel brought home by a strong north wind,

Your memory, as legends still unproven,
May, like a dulcimer, weary the mind,
And by some link for ever be entwined,
Fraternal, mystic, with my noble rhyme;

Accursed creature to whom none replies
But me, from deep abyss to highest skies!
– O thou, a shade with trace ephemeral,

Oppressing with light foot and gaze serene
Dull mortals who judged thee tyrannical,
Statue with eyes of jet, great angel with brass mien!

Tout entière

Le Démon, dans ma chambre haute,
Ce matin est venu me voir,
Et, tâchant à me prendre en faute,
Me dit : «Je voudrais bien savoir,

«Parmi toutes les belles choses
Dont est fait son enchantement,
Parmi les objets noirs ou roses
Qui composent son corps charmant,

«Quel est le plus doux.» – Ô mon âme!
Tu répondis à l'Abhorré :
«Puisqu'en Elle tout est dictame,
Rien ne peut être préféré.

«Lorsque tout me ravit, j'ignore
Si quelque chose me séduit.
Elle éblouit comme l'Aurore
Et console comme la Nuit;

«Et l'harmonie est trop exquise,
Qui gouverne tout son beau corps,
Pour que l'impuissante analyse
En note les nombreux accords.

«Ô métamorphose mystique
De tous mes sens fondus en un!
Son haleine fait la musique,
Comme sa voix fait le parfum!»

Entire

The Devil, in my upper room,
Arrived to visit me today,
And, bent on machination,
Said to me: 'Tell me this, I pray:

Among the beauties numerous
Of which her sorcery is made,
Among the features black and rose
In all her body dear displayed,

Which is the sweetest?' – O my soul!
This you replied to the Abhorred:
'Since all things in Her do console,
No one of them can be preferred.

All things enchant, I know not one
That gives particular delight.
She dazzles brilliant as the Dawn,
And she consoles me like the Night.

It is too fine a harmony
That rules her body exquisite
For rough analysis to try
To register its every note.

O mystic metamorphosis
Of all my senses merged in one!
Her breath echoes like symphonies,
Her voice is balm elysian!'

«Que diras-tu ce soir, pauvre âme solitaire . . .»

Que diras-tu ce soir, pauvre âme solitaire,
Que diras-tu, mon cœur, cœur autrefois flétri,
À la très-belle, à la très-bonne, à la très-chère,
Dont le regard divin t'a soudain refleuri?

– Nous mettrons notre orgueil à chanter ses louanges:
Rien ne vaut la douceur de son autorité;
Sa chair spirituelle a le parfum des Anges,
Et son œil nous revêt d'un habit de clarté.

Que ce soit dans la nuit et dans la solitude,
Que ce soit dans la rue et dans la multitude,
Son fantôme dans l'air danse comme un flambeau.

Parfois il parle et dit: «Je suis belle, et j'ordonne
Que pour l'amour de moi vous n'aimiez que le Beau;
Je suis l'Ange gardien, la Muse et la Madone.»

'What will you say tonight, poor lonesome soul . . .'

What will you say tonight, poor lonesome soul,
What will you say, my heart, my heart once dead,
To the most dear, the best, most beautiful,
Beneath whose glance divine you blossomed?

– We shall be proud her name to magnify:
Her sweet authority is more than all;
Her spiritual flesh breathes sanctity,
Her eyes robe us in garb celestial.

Be it in darkness and in solitude,
Or in the street, among the multitude,
Her beacon-spirit dances in the air.

Sometimes it tells me: 'I am beautiful,
For my sake, you must only love the fair;
I am Muse, goddess, guide angelical.'

Le Flambeau vivant

Ils marchent devant moi, ces Yeux pleins de lumières,
Qu'un Ange très-savant a sans doute aimantés;
Ils marchent, ces divins frères qui sont mes frères,
Secouant dans mes yeux leurs feux diamantés.

Me sauvant de tout piège et de tout péché grave,
Ils conduisent mes pas dans la route du Beau;
Ils sont mes serviteurs et je suis leur esclave;
Tout mon être obéit à ce vivant flambeau.

Charmants Yeux, vous brillez de la clarté mystique
Qu'ont les cierges brûlant en plein jour; le soleil
Rougit, mais n'éteint pas leur flamme fantastique;

Ils célèbrent la Mort, vous chantez le Réveil;
Vous marchez en chantant le réveil de mon âme,
Astres dont nul soleil ne peut flétrir la flamme!

The Living Flame

They go before me, Eyes most radiant,
No doubt magnetic made by Angels wise,
They go, these heavenly kin which are my kin,
And cast their diamond brightness in my eyes.

They keep me from all snare and trespass grave,
They guide my steps towards the Beautiful;
They are my servants and I am their slave;
This living flame I follow heart and soul.

Enchanting Eyes, you have the mystic light
Of candles burning at high noon; the sun
Reddens, but does not pale their strangeness bright;

They sing of Death, you sing the Resurrection;
You sing the Resurrection of my soul,
Bright stars whose brilliance no sun can dull!

Réversibilité

Ange plein de gaîté, connaissez-vous l'angoisse,
La honte, les remords, les sanglots, les ennuis,
Et les vagues terreurs de ces affreuses nuits
Qui compriment le cœur comme un papier qu'on froisse?
Ange plein de gaîté, connaissez-vous l'angoisse?

Ange plein de bonté, connaissez-vous la haine,
Les poings crispés dans l'ombre et les larmes de fiel,
Quand la Vengeance bat son infernal rappel,
Et de nos facultés se fait le capitaine?
Ange plein de bonté, connaissez-vous la haine?

Ange plein de santé, connaissez-vous les Fièvres,
Qui, le long des grands murs de l'hospice blafard,
Comme des exilés, s'en vont d'un pied traînard,
Cherchant le soleil rare et remuant les lèvres?
Ange plein de santé, connaissez-vous les Fièvres?

Ange plein de beauté, connaissez-vous les rides,
Et la peur de vieillir, et ce hideux tourment
De lire la secrète horreur du dévouement
Dans des yeux où longtemps burent nos yeux avides?
Ange plein de beauté, connaissez-vous les rides?

Ange plein de bonheur, de joie et de lumières,
David mourant aurait demandé la santé
Aux émanations de ton corps enchanté;
Mais de toi je n'implore, ange, que tes prières,
Ange plein de bonheur, de joie et de lumières!

Reversibility

Angel so gay, know you the misery,
The shame, the weeping, the remorse, the grief,
The vague fears of those nights beyond belief
Which crumple up the heart's security?
Angel so gay, know you the misery?

Angel so good, know you aversion,
The fists clenched in the dark, the bitter tears,
When Vengeance calls its hellish volunteers,
And comes to captain our decision?
Angel so good, know you aversion?

Angel so healthy, know you maladies,
Which, down the vast walls of dim hospitals,
Like exiles, drag their way rheumatical,
Seeking rare sun, mouthing inaudibly?
Angel so healthy, know you maladies?

Angel so lovely, know you greying hair,
The fear of age, this desolation
Of reading horror of devotion
In eyes which long fulfilled our ardent prayer?
Angel so lovely, know you greying hair?

Angel so happy, joyful, radiant,
The dying David would have asked to live
By the enchantment that your body gives;
But I for prayers alone am supplicant,
Angel so happy, joyful, radiant!

L'Aube spirituelle

Quand chez les débauchés l'aube blanche et vermeille
Entre en société de l'Idéal rongeur,
Par l'opération d'un mystère vengeur
Dans la brute assoupie un ange se réveille.

Des Cieux Spirituels l'inaccessible azur,
Pour l'homme terrassé qui rêve encore et souffre,
S'ouvre et s'enfonce avec l'attirance du gouffre.
Ainsi, chère Déesse, Être lucide et pur,

Sur les débris fumeux des stupides orgies
Ton souvenir plus clair, plus rose, plus charmant,
À mes yeux agrandis voltige incessamment.

Le soleil a noirci la flamme des bougies;
Ainsi, toujours vainqueur, ton fantôme est pareil,
Âme resplendissante, à l'immortel soleil!

The Spiritual Dawn

When white and rosy dawn to rakes appears
With the Ideal that ever gnaws away,
By some strange and avenging agency
Within the sleeping brute an angel stirs.

The man afflicted who dreams on in pain
Sees the remote and Spiritual Skies
Open alluring, deep as the abyss.
So, lovely goddess, bright and heaven-born,

Upon the smoky débris of excess
Your memory more charming, roseate, bright,
Hovers without end in my eager sight.

The sunlight does the candlelight surpass;
So, ever conquering, your benison,
Resplendent soul, is like the deathless sun!

Harmonie du soir

Voici venir les temps où vibrant sur sa tige
Chaque fleur s'évapore ainsi qu'un encensoir;
Les sons et les parfums tournent dans l'air du soir;
Valse mélancolique et langoureux vertige!

Chaque fleur s'évapore ainsi qu'un encensoir;
Le violon frémit comme un cœur qu'on afflige;
Valse mélancolique et langoureux vertige!
Le ciel est triste et beau comme un grand reposoir.

Le violon frémit comme un cœur qu'on afflige,
Un cœur tendre, qui hait le néant vaste et noir!
Le ciel est triste et beau comme un grand reposoir;
Le soleil s'est noyé dans son sang qui se fige.

Un cœur tendre qui hait le néant vaste et noir,
Du passé lumineux recueille tout vestige!
Le soleil s'est noyé dans son sang qui se fige . . .
Ton souvenir en moi luit comme un ostensoir!

Evening Harmony

Behold the times when trembling on their stems
The flowers evaporate like thuribles;
The sounds and scents turn in the evening cool;
Sad waltz, languid intoxication!

The flowers evaporate like thuribles;
The viol quivers like a heart that's torn;
Sad waltz, languid intoxication!
The sky is sad like some memorial.

The viol quivers like a heart that's torn,
A heart that hates the void perpetual!
The sky is sad like some memorial;
The sun has drowned in its vermilion.

A heart that hates the void perpetual
Recalls each glowing moment of times gone!
The sun has drowned in its vermilion . . .
Your memory shines, my monstrance personal.

Ciel brouillé

On dirait ton regard d'une vapeur couvert;
Ton œil mystérieux (est-il bleu, gris ou vert?)
Alternativement tendre, rêveur, cruel,
Réfléchit l'indolence et la pâleur du ciel.

Tu rappelles ces jours blancs, tièdes et voilés,
Qui font se fondre en pleurs les cœurs ensorcelés,
Quand, agités d'un mal inconnu qui les tord,
Les nerfs trop éveillés raillent l'esprit qui dort.

Tu ressembles parfois à ces beaux horizons
Qu'allument les soleils des brumeuses saisons . . .
Comme tu resplendis, paysage mouillé
Qu'enflamment les rayons tombant d'un ciel brouillé!

Ô femme dangereuse, ô séduisants climats!
Adorerai-je aussi ta neige et vos frimas,
Et saurai-je tirer de l'implacable hiver
Des plaisirs plus aigus que la glace et le fer?

Troubled Sky

Your gaze appears with vapours overcast;
Blue, grey or green? Your eyes mysterious,
Pensive or tender or tyrannical,
Reflect the indolence of heaven pale.

You bring to mind those white, warm, misty hours,
Which make the spellbound heart dissolve in tears,
When, troubled by pain indefinable,
The nerves, too wakeful, mock the sleeping soul.

And you are sometimes like horizons fine
Illumined by the suns of autumn time . . .
Wet landscape, shimmering resplendently,
Lit up by sunshine from a troubled sky!

O woman perilous, alluring climes!
O, shall I worship, too, your snow and rime,
And in your wintertime implacable
Discover sharper joys than ice and steel?

L'Invitation au voyage

> Mon enfant, ma sœur,
> Songe à la douceur
> D'aller là-bas vivre ensemble!
> Aimer à loisir,
> Aimer et mourir
> Au pays qui te ressemble!
> Les soleils mouillés
> De ces ciels brouillés
> Pour mon esprit ont les charmes
> Si mystérieux
> De tes traîtres yeux
> Brillant à travers leurs larmes.
>
> Là, tout n'est qu'ordre et beauté,
> Luxe, calme et volupté.
>
> Des meubles luisants,
> Polis par les ans,
> Décoreraient notre chambre;
> Les plus rares fleurs
> Mêlant leurs odeurs
> Aux vagues senteurs de l'ambre,
> Les riches plafonds,
> Les miroirs profonds,
> La splendeur orientale,
> Tout y parlerait
> À l'âme en secret
> Sa douce langue natale.
>
> Là, tout n'est qu'ordre et beauté,
> Luxe, calme et volupté.
>
> Vois sur ces canaux
> Dormir ces vaisseaux

Invitation to a Journey

My sister, my sweet,
    Think of the delight
Of journeying to live together there!
    To love leisurely,
    To love and to die
In lands to which you seem so similar!
    The watery suns
    In troubled heavens
Have for my soul the charms beyond compare,
    So mysterious,
    Of your faithless eyes,
When they shine resplendent through their tears.

There, all is loveliness and harmony,
Enchantment, pleasure and serenity.

    Gleaming furniture,
    Polished by the years,
Would, rich and lambent, decorate our room;
    And flowers most rare
    Would mingle attar
With bergamot and amber's vague perfume;
    Rich ceilings adorned
    And mirrors profound,
Magnificence and splendour of the East:
    All of them would speak
    To our souls, oblique,
The language sweet they understand the best.

There, all is loveliness and harmony,
Enchantment, pleasure and serenity.

    See on the canals
    The ships with furled sails

Dont l'humeur est vagabonde;
    C'est pour assouvir
    Ton moindre désir
Qu'ils viennent du bout du monde.
    – Les soleils couchants
    Revêtent les champs,
Les canaux, la ville entière,
    D'hyacinthe et d'or;
    Le monde s'endort
Dans une chaude lumière.

Là, tout n'est qu'ordre et beauté,
Luxe, calme et volupté.

Whose inclination is vagabond;
    It is but to grant
    Your every want
That they have journeyed here from the world's end.
    – The low setting suns
    Paint all the champaigns,
And the canals, the city's whole expanse,
    In hyacinth, gold;
    And slumber enfolds
The universe in sultry brilliance.

There, all is loveliness and harmony,
Enchantment, pleasure and serenity.

L'Irréparable

i

Pouvons-nous étouffer le vieux, le long Remords,
    Qui vit, s'agite et se tortille,
Et se nourrit de nous comme le ver des morts,
    Comme du chêne la chenille?
Pouvons-nous étouffer l'implacable Remords?

Dans quel philtre, dans quel vin, dans quelle tisane,
    Noierons-nous ce vieil ennemi,
Destructeur et gourmand comme la courtisane,
    Patient comme la fourmi?
Dans quel philtre? – dans quel vin? – dans quelle tisane?

Dis-le, belle sorcière, oh! dis, si tu le sais,
    À cet esprit comblé d'angoisse
Et pareil au mourant qu'écrasent les blessés,
    Que le sabot du cheval froisse,
Dis-le, belle sorcière, oh! dis, si tu le sais,

À cet agonisant que le loup déjà flaire
    Et que surveille le corbeau,
À ce soldat brisé! s'il faut qu'il désespère
    D'avoir sa croix et son tombeau;
Ce pauvre agonisant que déjà le loup flaire!

Peut-on illuminer un ciel bourbeux et noir?
    Peut-on déchirer des ténèbres
Plus denses que la poix, sans matin et sans soir,
    Sans astres, sans éclairs funèbres?
Peut-on illuminer un ciel bourbeux et noir?

L'Espérance qui brille aux carreaux de l'Auberge
    Est soufflée, est morte à jamais!

The Irreparable

Can we make silent old and long Remorse,
    Which lives and writhes and moves
And feeds on us as worms feed on a corpse,
    As grubs on verdant groves?
Can we make silent old and long Remorse?

What philtre, wine, infusion will drown
    This ancient combatant,
Destructive, greedy like the courtesan,
    Unswerving like the ant?
What philtre, wine, infusion will drown?

Tell me, fair sorceress, I beg you, tell
    This spirit in distress,
And like the dying man left on the field,
    Bruised as the horses pass,
Tell me, fair sorceress, I beg you, tell

This dying man the wolf already smells,
    The crow sees, ominous,
This broken soldier: must he bid farewell
    To hopes of tomb and cross?
This dying man the wolf already smells?

Can one light up the dark and troubled skies
    Or tear apart the gloom
More dense than pitch, where no suns set or rise,
    No stars exist, no gleam?
Can one light up the dark and troubled skies?

Hope, shining at the windows of the Inn,
    Is snuffed out, ever dead!

Sans lune et sans rayons, trouver où l'on héberge
   Les martyrs d'un chemin mauvais!
Le Diable a tout éteint aux carreaux de l'Auberge!

Adorable sorcière, aimes-tu les damnés?
   Dis, connais-tu l'irrémissible?
Connais-tu le Remords, aux traits empoisonnés,
   À qui notre cœur sert de cible?
Adorable sorcière, aimes-tu les damnés?

L'Irréparable ronge, avec sa dent maudite
   Notre âme, piteux monument,
Et souvent il attaque, ainsi que le termite,
   Par la base le bâtiment.
L'Irréparable ronge avec sa dent maudite!

ii

– J'ai vu parfois, au fond d'un théâtre banal
   Qu'enflammait l'orchestre sonore,
Une fée allumer dans un ciel infernal
   Une miraculeuse aurore;
J'ai vu parfois au fond d'un théâtre banal

Un être, qui n'était que lumière, or et gaze,
   Terrasser l'énorme Satan;
Mais mon cœur, que jamais ne visite l'extase,
   Est un théâtre où l'on attend
Toujours, toujours en vain, l'Être aux ailes de gaze!

Moonless, unlit, where are they taken in,
   The martyrs of the road?
The Devil's put all lights out at the Inn!

Beloved Sorceress, love you the damned,
   The irremissible?
Know you Remorse, with poisoned arrows armed,
   Whose target is our soul?
Beloved sorceress, love you the damned?

Dejection with its cursed teeth consumes
   Our soul, sad citadel,
And often, like the termite-ant, it mines
   Beneath the very wall.
Dejection with its cursed teeth consumes!

ii

– I've sometimes seen, upon some stage banal,
   To music clamorous,
A fairy light up in the skies of Hell
   A dawn miraculous;
I've sometimes seen, upon some stage banal,

A creature, gold and gauze, all glimmering,
   Great Lucifer dismay;
In my own heart, which never rapture sings,
   I wait, await all day,
Always in vain, the creature with gauze wings!

Chant d'automne

i

Bientôt nous plongerons dans les froides ténèbres;
Adieu, vive clarté de nos étés trop courts!
J'entends déjà tomber avec des chocs funèbres
Le bois retentissant sur le pavé des cours.

Tout l'hiver va rentrer dans mon être: colère,
Haine, frissons, horreur, labeur dur et forcé,
Et, comme le soleil dans son enfer polaire,
Mon cœur ne sera plus qu'un bloc rouge et glacé.

J'écoute en frémissant chaque bûche qui tombe;
L'échafaud qu'on bâtit n'a pas d'écho plus sourd.
Mon esprit est pareil à la tour qui succombe
Sous les coups du bélier infatigable et lourd.

Il me semble, bercé par ce choc monotone,
Qu'on cloue en grande hâte un cercueil quelque part.
Pour qui? – C'était hier l'été; voici l'automne!
Ce bruit mystérieux sonne comme un départ.

ii

J'aime de vos longs yeux la lumière verdâtre,
Douce beauté, mais tout aujourd'hui m'est amer,
Et rien, ni votre amour, ni le boudoir, ni l'âtre,
Ne me vaut le soleil rayonnant sur la mer.

Et pourtant aimez-moi, tendre cœur! soyez mère,
Même pour un ingrat, même pour un méchant;
Amante ou sœur, soyez la douceur éphémère
D'un glorieux automne ou d'un soleil couchant.

Autumn Song

i

Soon we shall plunge into the shadows cold;
Farewell, the brilliance of brief summers gone!
Already I can hear the sad trees felled,
The wood resounding on the courtyard stone.

All winter will return into my soul:
Hate, anger, horror, toil, and sudden chill,
And, like the sun in its antarctic hell,
My heart, a red and frozen block, is still.

I listen, trembling, to each log that falls;
The scaffold being built echoes less dull.
My spirit broken like a citadel
By heavy battering-rams infallible.

I feel, lulled by these blows monotonous,
As if, quickly, a coffin were nailed down.
For whom? – Summer is dead; here autumn is!
This strange sound echoes as for someone gone.

ii

I love the greenish light of your long eyes,
Sweet beauty, but today all saddens me,
No love or hearth or boudoir satisfies
My soul like radiant sunshine on the sea.

Yet love me, tender heart! A mother be,
Though for a sinner, for a thankless man;
Be mistress, sister, sweetness transitory
Of splendid autumn or of setting sun.

Courte tâche! La tombe attend; elle est avide!
Ah! laissez-moi, mon front posé sur vos genoux,
Goûter, en regrettant l'été blanc et torride,
De l'arrière-saison le rayon jaune et doux!

Brief task! The grave awaits me, avidly!
O let me on your lap my head incline,
Lament the incandescent summer day,
Savour the golden sweetness of decline.

À une Madone

EX-VOTO DANS LE GOÛT ESPAGNOL

Je veux bâtir pour toi, Madone, ma maîtresse,
Un autel souterrain au fond de ma détresse,
Et creuser dans le coin le plus noir de mon cœur,
Loin du désir mondain et du regard moqueur,
Une niche, d'azur et d'or tout émaillée,
Où tu te dresseras, Statue émerveillée.
Avec mes vers polis, treillis d'un pur métal
Savamment constellé de rimes de cristal,
Je ferai pour ta tête une énorme Couronne;
Et dans ma Jalousie, ô mortelle Madone,
Je saurai te tailler un Manteau, de façon
Barbare, roide et lourd, et doublé de soupçon,
Qui, comme une guérite, enfermera tes charmes;
Non de Perles brodé, mais de toutes mes Larmes!
Ta Robe, ce sera mon Désir, frémissant,
Onduleux, mon Désir qui monte et qui descend,
Aux pointes se balance, aux vallons se repose,
Et revêt d'un baiser tout ton corps blanc et rose.
Je te ferai de mon Respect de beaux Souliers
De satin, par tes pieds divins humiliés,
Qui, les emprisonnant dans une molle étreinte,
Comme un moule fidèle en garderont l'empreinte.
Si je ne puis, malgré tout mon art diligent,
Pour Marchepied tailler une Lune d'argent,
Je mettrai le Serpent qui me mord les entrailles
Sous tes talons, afin que tu foules et railles,
Reine victorieuse et féconde en rachats,
Ce monstre tout gonflé de haine et de crachats.
Tu verras mes Pensers, rangés comme les Cierges
Devant l'autel fleuri de la Reine des Vierges,
Étoilant de reflets le plafond peint en bleu,
Te regarder toujours avec des yeux de feu;

To a Madonna

EX-VOTO IN THE SPANISH STYLE

I want to build for you, Madonna, you, o mistress mine,
A hidden altar in the depths of my affliction,
And hollow out in the most sombre corner of my soul,
Far from the world's desire and from observers cynical,
A niche, enamelled perfectly with azure and with gold,
Where you, my Statue, stand in your astonishment untold.
With brilliant Lines drawn by my pen, trellis of metal fine,
Embellished – cunning exquisite! – with stars of crystal rhyme,
I shall make for your head a Crown of towering majesty,
And o Madonna mortal, in my mortal jealousy
I shall contrive to fashion you a Mantle in a style
Barbaric, heavy, stiff, and lined with doubt incredible,
A Mantle like a belvedere which will your charms confine;
And not with Pearls embroidered, but with every Tear of mine!
As for your Robe: your Robe shall be my tremulous Desire,
Enveloping Desire which grows, advances and retires,
Upon the headlands hovers, in the valleys seeks repose,
And dresses all your body white and roseate with a kiss.
I shall make you from my Respect a pair of Slippers fine,
Of satin, that they may be humbled by your feet divine,
And, guarding them as prisoners within their gentle hold,
They will for ever keep their imprint like a faithful mould.
If I cannot, for all my art and all my diligence,
Cut out a silver Moon for Footstool in my reverence,
Then I shall put the Serpent which my entrails eats away
Beneath your feet, so that you trample down, in mockery,
Sovereign victorious, full of redemption,
This monster all swelled up with spit and detestation.
You will see my Thoughts set out: like Candles tall which burn
Before the altar decked with flowers of the Virgin Queen,
Starring the ceiling, painted blue, with their reflection,
And gazing at you constantly with adoration;

Et comme tout en moi te chérit et t'admire,
Tout se fera Benjoin, Encens, Oliban, Myrrhe,
Et sans cesse vers toi, sommet blanc et neigeux,
En Vapeurs montera mon Esprit orageux.

Enfin, pour compléter ton rôle de Marie,
Et pour mêler l'amour avec la barbarie,
Volupté noire! des sept Péchés capitaux,
Bourreau plein de remords, je ferai sept Couteaux
Bien affilés, et, comme un jongleur insensible,
Prenant le plus profond de ton amour pour cible,
Je les planterai tous dans ton cœur pantelant,
Dans ton Cœur sanglotant, dans ton Cœur ruisselant!

And as all within me worships you and holds you dear,
All will turn to Benzoin, Incense, Frankincense and Myrrh,
And towards you, summit snowy-white and wonderful,
Will rise in vapours never-ending my tempestuous Soul.

And so that you fulfil your rôle of Mary perfectly,
So that at last I mingle passion with barbarity,
O sombre ravishment! I shall the seven deadly Sins,
Remorseful torturer, turn into seven javelins
Well honed and sharpened, and – a juggler skilled and passionless –
I shall take aim, and make my target all your love's largesse,
And I shall plant each one of them where you most feel the hurt,
Within your sobbing, breaking Heart, within your streaming Heart.

À une Dame créole

Au pays parfumé que le soleil caresse,
J'ai connu, sous un dais d'arbres tout empourprés
Et de palmiers d'où pleut sur les yeux la paresse,
Une dame créole aux charmes ignorés.

Son teint est pâle et chaud; la brune enchanteresse
A dans le cou des airs noblement maniérés;
Grande et svelte en marchant comme une chasseresse,
Son sourire est tranquille et ses yeux assurés.

Si vous alliez, Madame, au vrai pays de gloire,
Sur les bords de la Seine ou de la verte Loire,
Belle digne d'orner les antiques manoirs,

Vous feriez, à l'abri des ombreuses retraites,
Germer mille sonnets dans le cœur des poëtes,
Que vos grands yeux rendraient plus soumis que vos noirs.

To a Creole Woman

In aromatic lands loved by the sun,
Beneath empurpled canopies of trees,
And palm-trees which an indolence rain down,
I knew a creole's haunting mysteries.

Her skin is pale and warm; enchantress brown,
She holds her head with nobly mannered ease;
She walks tall, slender like an amazon,
Her smile serene, assurance in her gaze.

If you, Madame, went to the very scene
Of glory, by the green Loire or the Seine,
To ornament some manor ancient,

Shadowed by these retreats of shadows full,
You'd sow a thousand sonnets in men's souls:
Made by your eyes, like slaves, obedient.

Mœsta et Errabunda

Dis-moi, ton cœur parfois s'envole-t-il, Agathe,
Loin du noir océan de l'immonde cité,
Vers un autre océan où la splendeur éclate,
Bleu, clair, profond, ainsi que la virginité?
Dis-moi, ton cœur parfois s'envole-t-il, Agathe?

La mer, la vaste mer, console nos labeurs!
Quel démon a doté la mer, rauque chanteuse
Qu'accompagne l'immense orgue des vents grondeurs,
De cette fonction sublime de berceuse?
La mer, la vaste mer, console nos labeurs!

Emporte-moi, wagon! enlève-moi, frégate!
Loin, loin! ici la boue est faite de nos pleurs!
– Est-il vrai que parfois le triste cœur d'Agathe
Dise: Loin des remords, des crimes, des douleurs,
Emporte-moi, wagon, enlève-moi, frégate?

Comme vous êtes loin, paradis parfumé,
Où sous un clair azur tout n'est qu'amour et joie,
Où tout ce que l'on aime est digne d'être aimé,
Où dans la volupté pure le cœur se noie!
Comme vous êtes loin, paradis parfumé!

Mais le vert paradis des amours enfantines,
Les courses, les chansons, les baisers, les bouquets,
Les violons vibrant derrière les collines,
Avec les brocs de vin, le soir, dans les bosquets,
– Mais le vert paradis des amours enfantines,

L'innocent paradis, plein de plaisirs furtifs,
Est-il déjà plus loin que l'Inde et que la Chine?
Peut-on le rappeler avec des cris plaintifs,
Et l'animer encor d'une voix argentine,
L'innocent paradis plein de plaisirs furtifs?

Mœsta et Errabunda

Say, Agatha, does your spirit sometimes wing
Far from the unclean city's sombre sea,
Towards a splendid ocean shimmering
Blue, deep and lucid, like virginity?
Say, Agatha, does your spirit sometimes wing?

The sea, the vast sea, comforts us for toil!
What demon gave that singer harsh, the sea,
With its immense and organ-roaring winds,
The sacred function of a lullaby?
The sea, the vast sea, comforts us for toil!

Waggon or frigate, carry me away,
Far, far away! Our mud is made of tears!
– Does Agatha's sad spirit sometimes say:
Far from remorse, from wickedness and cares,
Waggon or frigate, carry me away?

How far you are, o fragrant paradise,
Where under heaven all is love and joy,
Where all one loves the loving justifies,
The heart is lost in bliss without alloy!
How far you are, o fragrant paradise!

But the green paradise of childhood loves,
The rides, the kisses, flowers and madrigals,
The jugs of wine, at evening, in the groves,
The violins trembling behind the hills,
– But the green paradise of childhood loves,

The artless paradise of timid bliss,
Is it already gone beyond Cathay?
And can one call it back with plaintive cries,
Give it new life, its silver words to say,
The artless paradise of timid bliss?

Le Revenant

Comme les anges à l'œil fauve,
Je reviendrai dans ton alcôve
Et vers toi glissera sans bruit
Avec les ombres de la nuit;

Et je te donnerai, ma brune,
Das baisers froids comme la lune
Et des caresses de serpent
Autour d'une fosse rampant.

Quand viendra le matin livide,
Tu trouveras ma place vide,
Où jusqu'au soir il fera froid.

Comme d'autres par la tendresse,
Sur ta vie et sur ta jeunesse,
Moi, je veux régner par l'effroi.

The Ghost

Like an angel wild of eye,
I shall return to where you lie
And towards you, noiseless, glide
With the shades of eventide.

I shall give you, dusky one,
Kisses icy as the moon,
Embraces that a snake would give
As it crawled around a grave.

When the sombre morning comes
You will find your lover gone,
My place cold till the night draws near.

As others reign through tenderness,
Over your life and youthfulness,
I want, myself, to reign through fear.

Tristesses de la lune

Ce soir, la lune rêve avec plus de paresse;
Ainsi qu'une beauté, sur de nombreux coussins,
Qui d'une main discrète et légère caresse
Avant de s'endormir le contour de ses seins,

Sur le dos satiné des molles avalanches,
Mourante, elle se livre aux longues pâmoisons,
Et promène ses yeux sur les visions blanches
Qui montent dans l'azur comme des floraisons.

Quand parfois sur ce globe, en sa langueur oisive,
Elle laisse filer une larme furtive,
Un poëte pieux, ennemi du sommeil,

Dans le creux de sa main prend cette larme pâle,
Aux reflets irisés comme un fragment d'opale,
Et la met dans son cœur loin des yeux du soleil.

Sorrows of the Moon

This evening the moon dreams more lazily;
As some fair woman, lost in cushions deep,
With gentle hand caresses listlessly
The contour of her breasts before she sleeps,

On velvet backs of avalanches soft
She often lies enraptured as she dies,
And gazes on white visions aloft
Which like a blossoming to heaven rise.

When sometimes on this globe, in indolence,
She lets a secret tear drop down, by chance,
A poet, set against oblivion,

Takes in his hand this pale and furtive tear,
This opal drop where rainbow hues appear,
And hides it in his breast far from the sun.

Les Chats

Les amoureux fervents et les savants austères
Aiment également, dans leur mûre saison,
Les chats puissants et doux, orgueil de la maison,
Qui comme eux sont frileux et comme eux sédentaires.

Amis de la science et de la volupté,
Ils cherchent le silence et l'horreur des ténèbres;
L'Érèbe les eût pris pour ses coursiers funèbres,
S'ils pouvaient au servage incliner leur fierté.

Ils prennent en songeant les nobles attitudes
Des grands sphinx allongés au fond des solitudes,
Qui semblent s'endormir dans un rêve sans fin;

Leurs reins féconds sont pleins d'étincelles magiques,
Et des parcelles d'or, ainsi qu'un sable fin,
Étoilent vaguement leurs prunelles mystiques.

The Cats

Lovers most passionate, scholars austere
Both love, when their autumnal season falls,
Strong, gentle cats, majestic, beautiful;
They, too, sit still, and feel the cold night air.

The friends of learning and of ecstasy,
They seek the silence of forbidding shades;
Hell would have chosen them as sombre steeds
If they were not too proud for slavery.

They dream and take the noble attitudes
Of sphinxes lazing in deep solitudes,
Which seem to slumber in an endless dream;

Their fecund loins of magic sparks are full,
And, like a fine sand, gold scintillas gleam
And vaguely star their pupils mystical.

Les Hiboux

Sous les ifs noirs qui les abritent,
Les hiboux se tiennent rangés,
Ainsi que les dieux étrangers,
Dardant leur œil rouge. Ils méditent.

Sans remuer ils se tiendront
Jusqu'à l'heure mélancolique
Où, poussant le soleil oblique,
Les ténèbres s'établiront.

Leur attitude au sage enseigne
Qu'il faut en ce monde qu'il craigne
Le tumulte et le mouvement;

L'homme ivre d'une ombre qui passe
Porte toujours le châtiment
D'avoir voulu changer de place.

The Owls

Beneath the sombre yew-trees' shade
The owls in solemn rows remain,
Like foreign deities profane,
Darting their scarlet eyes. They brood.

They will sit on there, motionless,
Until the sad time when day's done,
And, thrusting off the slanting sun,
The shadows will the world possess.

The wise man from their stance will learn
In his short life on earth to spurn
The vigorous and turbulent;

The men who passing shades embrace
Will always bear the punishment
For having wanted to change place.

La Musique

BEETHOVEN

La musique souvent me prend comme une mer!
　　　　Vers ma pâle étoile,
Sous un plafond de brume ou dans un vaste éther,
　　　　Je mets à la voile;

La poitrine en avant et les poumons gonflés
　　　　Comme de la toile,
J'escalade le dos des flots amoncelés
　　　　Que la nuit me voile;

Je sens vibrer en moi toutes les passions
　　　　D'un vaisseau qui souffre;
Le bon vent, la tempête et ses convulsions

　　　　Sur l'immense gouffre
Me bercent. D'autres fois, calme plat, grand miroir
　　　　De mon désespoir!

Music

BEETHOVEN

Music often takes me like a sea!
      To my star pale,
Beneath a hanging mist or boundless sky,
      I blithely sail;

Breast forward and my lungs swelled out with air,
      Like canvas full,
I scale the heights of waters gathered there
      Which darkness veils;

I feel pulsating all the passions:
      Ship in distress;
Fair wind, and storm and its commotions

      On the abyss
Rock me. At times dead calm, a vast reflection there
      Of my despair!

Le Mort joyeux

[LE SPLEEN]

Dans une terre grasse et pleine d'escargots
Je veux creuser moi-même une fosse profonde,
Où je puisse à loisir étaler mes vieux os
Et dormir dans l'oubli comme un requin dans l'onde.

Je hais les testaments et je hais les tombeaux;
Plutôt que d'implorer une larme du monde,
Vivant, j'aimerais mieux inviter les corbeaux
À saigner tous les bouts de ma carcasse immonde.

Ô vers! noirs compagnons sans oreille et sans yeux,
Voyez venir à vous un mort libre et joyeux;
Philosophes viveurs, fils de la pourriture,

À travers ma ruine allez donc sans remords,
Et dites-moi s'il est encor quelque torture
Pour ce vieux corps sans âme et mort parmi les morts!

Joyful Death

[SPLEEN]

In fertile earth, heavy and full of snails,
I want to dig myself a hollow grave,
And, leisurely, stretch out my mortal coil
And sleep, a shark forgotten in the waves.

I hate all testaments and funerals;
Rather than beg the world a tear to give,
I'd ask the crows to bleed my carcass foul
At all extremities while I still live.

O worms! Dark neighbours without eyes or ears,
Behold a free and joyful corpse appear;
Calm revellers, the offspring of decay,

Show no remorse, and on my ruin feed,
You may still give it some new agony:
This soulless corpse, old, dead among the dead!

La Cloche fêlée

[LE SPLEEN]

Il est amer et doux, pendant les nuits d'hiver,
D'écouter, près du feu qui palpite et qui fume,
Les souvenirs lointains lentement s'élever
Au bruit des carillons qui chantent dans la brume.

Bienheureuse la cloche au gosier vigoureux
Qui, malgré sa vieillesse, alerte et bien portante,
Jette fidèlement son cri religieux,
Ainsi qu'un vieux soldat qui veille sous la tente!

Moi, mon âme est fêlée, et lorsqu'en ses ennuis
Elle veut de ses chants peupler l'air froid des nuits,
Il arrive souvent que sa voix affaiblie

Semble le râle épais d'un blessé qu'on oublie
Au bord d'un lac de sang, sous un grand tas de morts,
Et qui meurt, sans bouger, dans d'immenses efforts.

The Cracked Bell

[SPLEEN]

Bitter and sweet it is, on winter eves,
To listen, as the fire smokes, flickering,
While dulled and distant memories revive
And, far across the mist, the church bells ring.

Happy the bell with accent vigorous
Which, aged though it be, is quick and well,
And still sends out its cry religious,
Like an old soldier standing sentinel!

My soul is cracked, and when in its despair
It wants its voice to fill the cold night air,
It often happens that its accents wan

Sound like the rattle of a wounded man
Left by a pool of blood, beneath the dead,
Who dies, quite still, his desperate struggle made.

Spleen

J'ai plus de souvenirs que si j'avais mille ans.

Un gros meuble à tiroirs encombré de bilans,
De vers, de billets doux, de procès, de romances,
Avec de lourds cheveux roulés dans des quittances,
Cache moins de secrets que mon triste cerveau.
C'est une pyramide, un immense caveau,
Qui contient plus de morts que la fosse commune.

– Je suis un cimetière abhorré de la lune,
Où comme des remords se traînent de longs vers
Qui s'acharnent toujours sur mes morts les plus chers.
Je suis un vieux boudoir plein de roses fanées,
Où gît tout un fouillis de modes surannées,
Où les pastels plaintifs et les pâles Boucher,
Seuls, respirent l'odeur d'un flacon débouché.

Rien n'égale en longueur les boiteuses journées,
Quand sous les lourds flocons des neigeuses années,
L'Ennui, fruit de la morne incuriosité,
Prend les proportions de l'immortalité.
– Désormais tu n'es plus, ô matière vivante!
Qu'un granit entouré d'une vague épouvante,
Assoupi dans le fond d'un Saharah brumeux;
Un vieux sphinx ignoré du monde insoucieux,
Oublié sur la carte, et dont l'humeur farouche
Ne chante qu'aux rayons du soleil qui se couche.

Spleen

I have more memories than a thousand years.

A chest-of-drawers cluttered with registers,
With poems, letters, songs, certificates,
With heavy locks of hair wrapped in receipts,
Hides fewer secrets than my mind forlorn.
It is a pyramid, a vast store-room
Which holds more dead than any sepulchres.

– I am a graveyard which the moon abhors,
Where, like regrets, the long worms ever crawl
And on my best loved hold their carnival.
I am a boudoir full of faded flowers,
Littered by fashions of other hours,
Where plaintive pastels, pale Bouchers alone
Breathe scent from bottles opened in days gone.

Nothing is so long as the halting hours,
When, burdened by the snowfall of the years,
Boredom, the fruit of dismal apathy,
Takes the proportions of eternity.
– Henceforth, o living world, you are no more
Than some old granite block hemmed in by fear,
Deep in Sahara misty sleeping on;
An old sphinx to a careless world unknown,
Forgotten on the map, whose dudgeon
Melts only in the warmth of setting suns!

Spleen

Je suis comme le roi d'un pays pluvieux,
Riche, mais impuissant, jeune et pourtant très-vieux,
Qui, de ses précepteurs méprisant les courbettes,
S'ennuie avec ses chiens comme avec d'autres bêtes.
Rien ne peut l'égayer, ni gibier, ni faucon,
Ni son peuple mourant en face du balcon.
Du bouffon favori la grotesque ballade
Ne distrait plus le front de ce cruel malade;
Son lit fleurdelisé se transforme en tombeau,
Et les dames d'atour, pour qui tout prince est beau,
Ne savent plus trouver d'impudique toilette
Pour tirer un souris de ce jeune squelette.
Le savant qui lui fait de l'or n'a jamais pu
De son être extirper l'élément corrompu,
Et dans ces bains de sang qui des Romains nous viennent,
Et dont sur leurs vieux jours les puissants se souviennent,
Il n'a su réchauffer ce cadavre hébété
Où coule au lieu de sang l'eau verte du Léthé.

Spleen

I am like the king of a rainy land,
Wealthy, but helpless, young and moribund,
Scorning his tutors fawning, plausible,
Weary of dogs and of other animals.
Nothing can cheer him, game or falconry,
His dying people by the balcony.
The monstrous ballad of the favourite fool
No longer makes him smile, cruel and ill.
His bed, with lilies decked, is now a tomb,
Tire-women who to every prince succumb
Can improvise no new and daring dress
To give this skeleton some happiness.
The sage who makes gold for him never could
Cut out the canker which his soul endued,
And in those blood-baths which gave Rome content,
And which great men recall when youth is spent,
He never could revive this corpse obtuse
In whom not blood but Lethe's water flows.

Spleen

Quand le ciel bas et lourd pèse comme un couvercle
Sur l'esprit gémissant en proie aux longs ennuis,
Et que de l'horizon embrassant tout le cercle
Il nous verse un jour noir plus triste que les nuits;

Quand la terre est changée en un cachot humide,
Où l'Espérance, comme une chauve-souris,
S'en va battant les murs de son aile timide
Et se cognant la tête à des plafonds pourris;

Quand la pluie étalant ses immenses traînées
D'une vaste prison imite les barreaux,
Et qu'un peuple muet d'infâmes araignées
Vient tendre ses filets au fond de nos cerveaux,

Des cloches tout à coup sautent avec furie
Et lancent vers le ciel un affreux hurlement,
Ainsi que des esprits errants et sans patrie
Qui se mettent à geindre opiniâtrement.

— Et de longs corbillards, sans tambours ni musique,
Défilent lentement dans mon âme; l'Espoir,
Vaincu, pleure, et l'Angoisse atroce, despotique,
Sur mon crâne incliné plante son drapeau noir.

Spleen

When, like a lid, the low and heavy sky
Weighs on the spirit burdened with long care,
And when, as far as mortal eye can see,
It sheds a darkness sadder than nights are;

When earth is changed into a prison cell,
Where, in the damp and dark, with timid wing
Hope, like a bat, goes beating at the wall,
Striking its head on ceilings mouldering;

When rain spreads out its never-ending trails
And imitates the bars of prisons vast,
And spiders, silent and detestable,
Crowd in, our minds with webs to overcast,

Some bells burst out in fury, suddenly,
And hurl a roar most terrible to heaven,
Like spirits lost for all eternity
Who start, most obstinately, to complain.

And, without drums or music, funerals
File past, in slow procession, in my soul;
Hope weeps, defeated; Pain, tyrannical,
Atrocious, plants its black flag on my skull.

Obsession

Grands bois, vous m'effrayez comme des cathédrales;
Vous hurlez comme l'orgue; et dans nos cœurs maudits,
Chambres d'éternel deuil où vibrent de vieux râles,
Répondent les échos de vos *De profundis*.

Je te hais, Océan! tes bonds et tes tumultes,
Mon esprit les retrouve en lui; ce rire amer
De l'homme vaincu, plein de sanglots et d'insultes,
Je l'entends dans le rire énorme de la mer.

Comme tu me plairais, ô nuit! sans ces étoiles
Dont la lumière parle un langage connu!
Car je cherche le vide, et le noir, et le nu!

Mais les ténèbres sont elles-mêmes des toiles
Où vivent, jaillissant de mon œil par milliers,
Des êtres disparus aux regards familiers.

Obsession

Great woods, cathedral-like, you frighten me;
You roar like organs; in our cursed hearts,
Death-chambers vibrant with old agony,
Your *De profundis* finds its counterpart.

I hate you, Ocean! Your storm and stir
My spirit knows; the bitter gaiety
Of man defeated, full of insults, tears,
I hear in the vast laughter of the sea.

How you would please me, night! without those stars
Whose brilliance speaks a language understood!
Because I seek the dark, the bare, the void!

And yet the very shadows pictures are,
Peopled with thousands whom my mind portrays,
Departed creatures with familiar gaze.

Le Couvercle

En quelque lieu qu'il aille, ou sur mer ou sur terre,
Sous un climat de flamme ou sous un soleil blanc,
Serviteur de Jésus, courtisan de Cythère,
Mendiant ténébreux ou Crésus rutilant,

Citadin, campagnard, vagabond, sédentaire,
Que son petit cerveau soit actif ou soit lent,
Partout l'homme subit la terreur du mystère,
Et ne regarde en haut qu'avec un œil tremblant.

En haut, le Ciel! ce mur de caveau qui l'étouffe,
Plafond illuminé par un opéra bouffe
Où chaque histrion foule un sol ensanglanté;

Terreur du libertin, espoir du fol ermite:
Le Ciel! couvercle noir de la grande marmite
Où bout l'imperceptible et vaste Humanité.

The Lid

Wherever he may go, on sea or land,
Under a sky of flame, or pallid sun,
Servant of Christ, or one of Venus' band,
Dark beggar, Croesus golden-bright as noon,

Town-dweller, oaf, untravelled, vagabond,
Whether of much intelligence or none,
Man always has the fear of the beyond,
And glances up with apprehension.

Above is heaven! Suffocating wall,
Ceiling lit up by opera comical
Where every actor treads on bloody ground;

Terror of libertines, and hermits' rest,
Heaven! The black lid of the cauldron vast
Where boils unseen, unnumbered, Humankind.

Madrigal triste

i

Que m'importe que tu sois sage?
Sois belle! et sois triste! Les pleurs
Ajoutent un charme au visage,
Comme le fleuve au paysage;
L'orage rajeunit les fleurs.

Je t'aime surtout quand la joie
S'enfuit de ton front terrassé;
Quand ton cœur dans l'horreur se noie;
Quand sur ton présent se déploie
Le nuage affreux du passé.

Je t'aime quand ton grand œil verse
Une eau chaude comme le sang;
Quand, malgré ma main qui te berce,
Ton angoisse, trop lourde, perce
Comme un râle d'agonisant.

J'aspire, volupté divine!
Hymne profond, délicieux!
Tous les sanglots de ta poitrine,
Et crois que ton cœur s'illumine
Des perles que versent tes yeux!

ii

Je sais que ton cœur, qui regorge
De vieux amours déracinés,
Flamboie encor comme une forge,
Et que tu couves sous ta gorge
Un peu de l'orgueil des damnés;

Sad Madrigal

i

What do I care if you are wise?
Be beautiful and sad! For tears
Add an enchantment to the eyes
Just as a river mirrors skies;
A storm revives the flowers.

I love you most when happiness
Deserts your countenance o'ercast;
When terrors do your heart oppress;
When, overhead, and ominous,
There spreads the dark cloud of the past.

I love you when your eyes let fall
A rain of tears as warm as blood;
When, though my hands caress and lull,
Your pain is irresistible,
Like moaning at infinitude.

I love, divine felicity!
Anthem profound and exquisite!
Your sobs, your heartfelt misery,
And think your heart shines brilliantly
With pearls shed by your eyes so bright!

ii

I know that now your heart still teems
With old uprooted passions;
Still, like a forge, it flares and flames,
And in your heart burns still, it seems,
The faint pride of damnation.

Mais tant, ma chère, que tes rêves
N'auront pas reflété l'Enfer,
Et qu'en un cauchemar sans trêves,
Songeant de poisons et de glaives,
Éprise de poudre et de fer,

N'ouvrant à chacun qu'avec crainte,
Déchiffrant le malheur partout,
Te convulsant quand l'heure tinte,
Tu n'auras pas senti l'étreinte
De l'irrésistible Dégoût,

Tu ne pourras, esclave reine
Qui ne m'aimes qu'avec effroi,
Dans l'horreur de la nuit malsaine
Me dire, l'âme de cris pleine:
«Je suis ton égale, ô mon Roi!»

But till your dreams, beloved one,
Have been reflections of Hell,
Till in a nightmare never done,
Thinking of poison, falchion,
In love with powder, shot and steel,

And opening to all with fear,
Seeking misfortune everywhere,
And stricken when the hour draws near,
You've been the helpless prisoner
Of irresistible Despair:

You won't be able, helot queen
Who loves me only quivering,
In the long horrid night obscene
To tell me, overcome with pain:
'I am your equal, o my King!'

Les Plaintes d'un Icare

Les amants des prostituées
Sont heureux, dispos et repus;
Quant à moi, mes bras sont rompus
Pour avoir étreint des nuées.

C'est grâce aux astres nonpareils,
Qui tout au fond du ciel flamboient,
Que mes yeux consumés ne voient
Que des souvenirs de soleils.

En vain j'ai voulu de l'espace
Trouver la fin et le milieu;
Sous je ne sais quel œil de feu
Je sens mon aile qui se casse;

Et brûlé par l'amour du beau,
Je n'aurai pas l'honneur sublime
De donner mon nom à l'abîme
Qui me servira de tombeau.

The Laments of an Icarus

The paramours of courtesans
Are well and satisfied, content;
But as for me, my limbs are rent
Because I clasped the clouds as mine.

I owe it to the peerless stars,
Which flame in the remotest sky,
That I see only, with spent eyes,
Remembered suns I knew before.

In vain I had at heart to find
The centre and the end of space;
Beneath some burning, unknown gaze
I feel my very wings unpinned.

And, burned because I beauty love,
I shall not know the highest bliss
And give my name to the abyss
Which waits to serve me as my grave.

Recueillement

Sois sage, ô ma Douleur, et tiens-toi plus tranquille.
Tu réclamais le Soir; il descend; le voici:
Une atmosphère obscure enveloppe la ville,
Aux uns portant la paix, aux autres le souci.

Pendant que des mortels la multitude vile,
Sous le fouet du Plaisir, ce bourreau sans merci,
Va cueillir des remords dans la fête servile,
Ma Douleur, donne-moi la main; viens par ici,

Loin d'eux. Vois se pencher les défuntes Années,
Sur les balcons du ciel, en robes surannées;
Surgir du fond des eaux le Regret souriant;

Le Soleil moribond s'endormir sous une arche,
Et, comme un long linceul traînant à l'Orient,
Entends, ma chère, entends la douce Nuit qui marche.

Meditation

Be wise, o my Affliction, be serene.
You called upon the Evening; now it falls:
Obscurity envelops all the town,
To some brings peace, to others brings ordeals.

While the vile multitude of common men,
Whipped on by unrelenting festivals,
Lay up regrets, like servile citizens,
Come you, Affliction, far from carnivals,

Give me your hand. See the dead Years lean down,
In dated dress, from balconies in heaven;
Behold Regret rise from the deep, unbowed;

The Sun sleep underneath an arch, and die,
And, trailing in the East, like a long shroud,
Listen, my dear: sweet Night walks through the sky.

L'Héautontimorouménos

À J. G. F.

Je te frapperai sans colère
Et sans haine, comme un boucher,
Comme Moïse le rocher!
Et je ferai de ta paupière,

Pour abreuver mon Saharah,
Jaillir les eaux de la souffrance.
Mon désir gonflé d'espérance
Sur tes pleurs salés nagera

Comme un vaisseau qui prend le large,
Et dans mon cœur qu'ils soûleront
Tes chers sanglots retentiront
Comme un tambour qui bat la charge!

Ne suis-je pas un faux accord
Dans la divine symphonie,
Grâce à la vorace Ironie
Qui me secoue et qui me mord?

Elle est dans ma voix, la criarde!
C'est tout mon sang, ce poison noir!
Je suis le sinistre miroir
Où la mégère se regarde.

Je suis la plaie et le couteau!
Je suis le soufflet et la joue!
Je suis les membres et la roue,
Et la victime et le bourreau!

The Heautontimoroumenos

To J. G. F.

I shall strike you without wrath
And, like a butcher, without hate,
Like Moses once in Horeb smote!
And there shall from your eyes spring forth,

To irrigate my desert dry,
The waters of affliction.
My desire with hope grown strong
On your salt tears will make its way

As vessels gain the open sea,
And in my heart inebriate
Your dear sobs will reverberate:
Drums urging onslaught on the enemy.

Am I not a discordant note
In the heaven's symphony,
Thanks to voracious Irony
Which devours and devastates?

It is in my voice, the scold,
It's all my blood, this hellebore,
I am the mirror sinister
In which the shrew herself beholds.

I am the dagger and the wound!
I am the blow, I am the cheek!
I am the body and the rack,
The torturer, the victim bound!

Je suis de mon cœur le vampire,
– Un de ces grands abandonnés
Au rire éternel condamnés,
Et qui ne peuvent plus sourire!

I am my vampire all the while,
– I'm one of those pariahs whose doom
Is laughing till the end of time,
Although they can no longer smile!

Tableaux Parisiens / Parisian Pictures

Paysage

Je veux, pour composer chastement mes églogues,
Coucher auprès du ciel, comme les astrologues,
Et, voisin des clochers, écouter en rêvant
Leurs hymnes solennels emportés par le vent.
Les deux mains au menton, du haut de ma mansarde,
Je verrai l'atelier qui chante et qui bavarde;
Les tuyaux, les clochers, ces mâts de la cité,
Et les grands ciels qui font rêver d'éternité.

Il est doux, à travers les brumes, de voir naître
L'étoile dans l'azur, la lampe à la fenêtre,
Les fleuves de charbon monter au firmament
Et la lune verser son pâle enchantement.
Je verrai les printemps, les étés, les automnes,
Et quand viendra l'hiver aux neiges monotones,
Je fermerai partout portières et volets
Pour bâtir dans la nuit mes féeriques palais.

Alors je rêverai des horizons bleuâtres,
Des jardins, des jets d'eau pleurant dans les albâtres,
Des baisers, des oiseaux chantant soir et matin,
Et tout ce que l'Idylle a de plus enfantin.
L'Émeute, tempêtant vainement à ma vitre,
Ne fera pas lever mon front de mon pupitre;
Car je serai plongé dans cette volupté
D'évoquer le Printemps avec ma volonté,
De tirer un soleil de mon cœur, et de faire
De mes pensers brûlants une tiède atmosphère.

Landscape

Since I would write my eclogues continent,
I must, seer-like, sleep near the firmament,
And, near the bell-towers, listen dreamily
As, on the wing, their anthems fade away.
From my high garret, chin in hands, I'll see
The workshop sing and chatter eagerly,
Chimneys and spires, masts of the capital,
And skies which make one dream of heaven and hell.

It's pleasant, through the mists, to see them born:
The star in heaven, lamplight in the room,
And watch the streams of smoke rise to the skies,
The moon pour forth its silver sorceries.
I'll see spring, summer, autumn tremulous;
When winter comes with snows monotonous,
With shutters, curtains, I'll keep out the light,
And build my magic castles in the night.

Then I shall dream of gardens, skylines blue,
Of fountains that from alabaster flow,
Of kisses, birds that sing at dusk and dawn,
And all that is idyllic, infantine.
Rebellion will rage outside in vain,
Still at my task, absorbed, I shall remain;
For I'll be lost in joy ineffable,
In summoning the Springtime at my will,
And, drawing sunshine from my heart, I'll try
To make my burning thoughts a sultry day.

Les petites Vieilles

À Victor Hugo

i

Dans les plis sinueux des vieilles capitales,
Où tout, même l'horreur, tourne aux enchantements,
Je guette, obéissant à mes humeurs fatales,
Des êtres singuliers, décrépits et charmants.

Ces monstres disloqués furent jadis des femmes,
Éponine ou Laïs! Monstres brisés, bossus
Ou tordus, aimons-les! ce sont encor des âmes.
Sous des jupons troués ou sous de froids tissus

Ils rampent, flagellés par les bises iniques,
Frémissant au fracas roulant des omnibus,
Et serrant sur leur flanc, ainsi que des reliques,
Un petit sac brodé de fleurs ou de rébus;

Ils trottent, tous pareils à des marionnettes;
Se traînent, comme font les animaux blessés,
Ou dansent, sans vouloir danser, pauvres sonnettes
Où se pend un Démon sans pitié! Tout cassés

Qu'ils sont, ils ont des yeux perçants comme une vrille,
Luisants comme ces trous où l'eau dort dans la nuit;
Ils ont les yeux divins de la petite fille
Qui s'étonne et qui rit à tout ce qui reluit.

– Avez-vous observé que maints cercueils de vieilles
Sont presque aussi petits que celui d'un enfant?
La Mort savante met dans ces bières pareilles
Un symbole d'un goût bizarre et captivant,

The Little Old Women

To Victor Hugo

i

In winding folds of ancient capitals,
Where all things have enchantment, even fear,
I wait, obeying humours whimsical,
To see frail creatures sweet and singular.

These broken souls were women long ago,
Laïs or Eponine! – Souls faded, bent
Or twisted: love them! They are still souls, now,
Beneath their cold clothes and their dresses rent.

They crawl, scourged by the criminal north wind,
Quake at the omnibuses' rumbling roar,
Hug to their side like sacred relics pinned
A purse embroidered with device or flower;

They trot along, as in a puppet show,
And drag themselves, like wounded animals,
Or dance a jig, whether they will or no,
Poor bells on which a cruel Demon pulls!

All broken as they are, their gimlet eyes
Shine like those holes where water sleeps at night;
They have the magic eyes of children shy
Who laugh, amazed, at everything that's bright.

– Have you seen? Many an old woman's bier
Is little bigger than that of a child.
Wise Death inspires these coffins similar;
Symbol engaging and unparalleled,

Et lorsque j'entrevois un fantôme débile
Traversant de Paris le fourmillant tableau,
Il me semble toujours que cet être fragile
S'en va tout doucement vers un nouveau berceau;

À moins que, méditant sur la géométrie,
Je ne cherche, à l'aspect de ces membres discords,
Combien de fois il faut que l'ouvrier varie
La forme de la boîte où l'on met tous ces corps.

– Ces yeux sont des puits faits d'un million de larmes,
Des creusets qu'un métal refroidi pailleta . . .
Ces yeux mystérieux ont d'invincibles charmes
Pour celui que l'austère infortune allaita!

ii

De Frascati défunt Vestale enamourée;
Prêtresse de Thalie, hélas! dont le souffleur
Enterré sait le nom; célèbre évaporée
Que Tivoli jadis ombragea dans sa fleur,

Toutes m'enivrent! mais parmi ces êtres frêles
Il en est qui, faisant de la douleur un miel,
Ont dit au Dévouement qui leur prêtait ses ailes:
Hippogriffe puissant, mène-moi jusqu'au ciel!

L'une, par sa patrie au malheur exercée,
L'autre, que son époux surchargea de douleurs,
L'autre, par son enfant Madone transpercée,
Toutes auraient pu faire un fleuve avec leurs pleurs!

iii

Ah! que j'en ai suivi de ces petites vieilles!
Une, entre autres, à l'heure où le soleil tombant
Ensanglante le ciel de blessures vermeilles,
Pensive s'asseyait à l'écart sur un banc,

And when I glimpse an unsubstantial ghost
Crossing the teeming scene Parisian,
I always feel this phantom from the past
Is gently going to a crib again;

Unless I'm thinking of geometry,
And judging, from these bodies dissonant,
How many different shapes it has to be,
The box which takes all creatures' measurement.

– These eyes are wells made of a million tears,
And crucibles starred by a metal cold . . .
These strange eyes have enchantments without peer
For one bred by Unhappiness untold!

ii

Vestal enamoured of Frascati's old,
Priestess of Thalia, whose prompter, dead,
Alone recalls her name: who, famous, strolled
In Tivoli, a golden giddy-head,

All these frail souls enrapture me! But some
Among them honey make from suffering,
And beg Devotion to bear them home:
'Great Hippogriff! For heaven lend me wings!'

One through her country knows all misery,
Another by her husband burdened sore,
A third, left by her child in agony,
All could have made a river of their tears!

iii

How often have I followed these poor souls!
Including one who, when the setting sun
The sky with bloody scarlet wounds despoils,
Pensive, upon a park bench sits alone,

Pour entendre un de ces concerts, riches de cuivre,
Dont les soldats parfois inondent nos jardins,
Et qui, dans ces soirs d'or où l'on se sent revivre,
Versent quelque héroïsme au cœur des citadins.

Celle-là, droite encor, fière et sentant la règle,
Humait avidement ce chant vif et guerrier;
Son œil parfois s'ouvrait comme l'œil d'un vieil aigle;
Son front de marbre avait l'air fait pour le laurier!

iv

Telles vous cheminez, stoïques et sans plaintes,
À travers le chaos des vivantes cités,
Mères au cœur saignant, courtisanes ou saintes,
Dont autrefois les noms par tous étaient cités.

Vous qui fûtes la grâce ou qui fûtes la gloire,
Nul ne vous reconnaît! un ivrogne incivil
Vous insulte en passant d'un amour dérisoire;
Sur vos talons gambade un enfant lâche et vil.

Honteuses d'exister, ombres ratatinées,
Peureuses, le dos bas, vous côtoyez les murs;
Et nul ne vous salue, étranges destinées!
Débris d'humanité pour l'éternité mûrs!

Mais moi, moi qui de loin tendrement vous surveille,
L'œil inquiet fixé sur vos pas incertains,
Tout comme si j'étais votre père, ô merveille!
Je goûte à votre insu des plaisirs clandestins:

Je vois s'épanouir vos passions novices;
Sombres ou lumineux, je vis vos jours perdus;
Mon cœur multiplié jouit de tous vos vices!
Mon âme resplendit de toutes vos vertus!

To hear one of those concerts, rich in brass,
Excessive, by some military band,
Which, on these evenings, gives new youthfulness,
Inspires the citizen with visions grand.

Poor soul, erect, and proud of discipline,
She avidly took in this martial song;
Her eyes were like an eagle's eyes at times;
Her marble brow to laurels did belong!

iv

So you go on, stoic, without complaints,
Amid the turmoil of the living town,
Mothers with bleeding hearts, street-walkers, saints,
Whose names were on the lips of everyone.

You who were once the glory or the grace,
Nobody knows you now! A drunk obscene
Passes, and casts derision in your face;
And at your heels run children coarse, unclean.

Ashamed to be alive, poor shrivelled ghosts,
Stooping and timorous, you hug the walls;
Nobody greets you, shades foredoomed and lost,
O human flotsam ripe for funerals!

But, from afar, I watch with tenderness,
My anxious eyes fixed on your steps unsure,
Just like a father; and, miraculous!
Unknown to you, new pleasures I explore:

I see the first bloom of your passions;
Dark, luminous, I see your vanished days;
My heart, now magnified, enjoys your sins!
My soul with all your virtues is ablaze!

Ruines! ma famille! ô cerveaux congénères!
Je vous fais chaque soir un solennel adieu!
Où serez-vous demain, Èves octogénaires,
Sur qui pèse la griffe effroyable de Dieu?

Ruins! My family! Minds like my own,
I bid you every night a last farewell!
Know you tomorrow, Eves of olden times,
Weighed down by God's own wrath implacable?

À une passante

La rue assourdissante autour de moi hurlait.
Longue, mince, en grand deuil, douleur majestueuse,
Une femme passa, d'une main fastueuse
Soulevant, balançant le feston et l'ourlet;

Agile et noble, avec sa jambe de statue.
Moi, je buvais, crispé comme un extravagant,
Dans son œil, ciel livide où germe l'ouragan,
La douceur qui fascine et le plaisir qui tue.

Un éclair . . . puis la nuit! – Fugitive beauté
Dont le regard m'a fait soudainement renaître,
Ne te verrai-je plus que dans l'éternité?

Ailleurs, bien loin d'ici! trop tard! *jamais* peut-être!
Car j'ignore où tu fuis, tu ne sais où je vais,
Ô toi que j'eusse aimée, ô toi qui le savais!

To a Passer-by

The street roared round me, deafening.
Tall, slender, in deep mourning, regal woe,
A woman passed, lifting her furbelow,
Holding her hem up, graceful, wondering;

Noble and lithe, her leg was sculptural.
And I myself, with wild intensity,
Drank in her eyes, a sombre, stormy sky,
The sweetness that enthrals, the joy that kills.

A lightning flash ... then night! Love passing by,
Whose sudden glance bestowed new life on me,
Shall I not see you till eternity?

But it's too far! Too late! *Never*, maybe!
I know not where you are – you, where I go,
You whom I should have loved – and felt it so!

«Je n'ai pas oublié, voisine de la ville . . .»

Je n'ai pas oublié, voisine de la ville,
Notre blanche maison, petite mais tranquille;
Sa Pomone de plâtre et sa vieille Vénus
Dans un bosquet chétif cachant leurs membres nus,
Et le soleil, le soir, ruisselant et superbe,
Qui, derrière la vitre où se brisait sa gerbe,
Semblait, grand œil ouvert dans le ciel curieux,
Contempler nos dîners longs et silencieux,
Répandant largement ses beaux reflets de cierge
Sur la nappe frugale et les rideaux de serge.

'I have not forgotten, near the town ...'

I have not forgotten, near the town,
Our little white house, peaceful and serene,
Its plaster Flora, Venus worn with time,
In meagre thicket hiding their bare limbs,
The splendid sun, at evening, streaming down,
Breaking its rays upon the window-pane:
A vast wide eye in the enquiring sky,
Observing our long dinners silently,
And spreading its fine glow like candlelight
Upon serge curtains, table temperate.

«*La servante au grand cœur dont vous étiez jalouse ...*»

La servante au grand cœur dont vous étiez jalouse,
Et qui dort son sommeil sous une humble pelouse,
Nous devrions pourtant lui porter quelques fleurs.
Les morts, les pauvres morts, ont de grandes douleurs,
Et quand octobre souffle, émondeur des vieux arbres,
Son vent mélancolique à l'entour de leurs marbres,
Certe, ils doivent trouver les vivants bien ingrats,
À dormir, comme ils font, chaudement dans leurs draps,
Tandis que, dévorés de noires songeries,
Sans compagnon de lit, sans bonnes causeries,
Vieux squelettes gelés travaillés par le ver,
Ils sentent s'égoutter les neiges de l'hiver
Et le siècle couler, sans qu'amis ni famille
Remplacent les lambeaux qui pendent à leur grille.

Lorsque la bûche siffle et chante, si le soir,
Calme, dans le fauteuil, je la voyais s'asseoir,
Si, par une nuit bleue et froide de décembre,
Je la trouvais tapie en un coin de ma chambre,
Grave, et venant du fond de son lit éternel
Couver l'enfant grandi de son œil maternel,
Que pourrais-je répondre à cette âme pieuse,
Voyant tomber des pleurs de sa paupière creuse?

'Great-hearted nurse who earned your jealousy . . .'

Great-hearted nurse who earned your jealousy:
Beneath the sward she sleeps on, quietly.
Yet we should take her flowers for times gone.
The poor dead know their desolation.
And when October, stripping ancient trees,
Blows, melancholy, round their cemeteries,
They must find living men ungrateful, then,
To sleep in warm beds when the day is done,
While they, devoured by their sombre dreams,
Without bedfellows, conversations,
Old frozen skeletons, a prey to worms,
Feel all the snows of wintertime drop down,
The years flow on – and no one comes to tend
The withered flowers: no relative or friend.

If, in the evening, by the singing fire,
I saw her sit down, peaceful, in her chair:
If, some December night of cold and gloom,
I found her in a corner of my room,
Pensive, arriving from eternity
To watch me, now a man, with mother's eyes,
What could I answer that Godfearing soul,
Seeing from hollow lids her tears fall?

Brumes et pluies

Ô fins d'automne, hivers, printemps trempés de boue,
Endormeuses saisons! je vous aime et vous loue
D'envelopper ainsi mon cœur et mon cerveau
D'un linceul vaporeux et d'un vague tombeau.

Dans cette grande plaine où l'autan froid se joue,
Où par les longues nuits la girouette s'enroue,
Mon âme mieux qu'au temps du tiède renouveau
Ouvrira largement ses ailes de corbeau.

Rien n'est plus doux au cœur plein de choses funèbres,
Et sur qui dès longtemps descendent les frimas,
Ô blafardes saisons, reines de nos climats,

Que l'aspect permanent de vos pâles ténèbres,
– Si ce n'est, par un soir sans lune, deux à deux,
D'endormir la douleur sur un lit hasardeux.

Mists and Rains

Late autumns, winters, springtimes steeped in mud,
You, drowsy seasons, earn my gratitude
For so enveloping my heart and mind
With vaporous winding-sheet, grave undefined.

On this vast plain where storms blow cold and rude,
Where weathercocks rust under hanging clouds,
My soul, more than in April, is inclined
To open wide its swart wings to the wind.

Nothing is sweeter to a mournful soul,
On whom the hoar-frost fell in distant times,
O sallow seasons, sovereigns of our climes,

Than seeing evermore your shadows pale,
– Unless, on moonless nights, and not alone,
On some chance bed one finds oblivion.

Le Crépuscule du matin

La diane chantait dans les cours des casernes,
Et le vent du matin soufflait sur les lanternes.

C'était l'heure où l'essaim des rêves malfaisants
Tord sur leurs oreillers les bruns adolescents;
Où, comme un œil sanglant qui palpite et qui bouge,
La lampe sur le jour fait une tache rouge;
Où l'âme, sous le poids du corps revêche et lourd,
Imite les combats de la lampe et du jour.
Comme un visage en pleurs que les brises essuient,
L'air est plein du frisson des choses qui s'enfuient,
Et l'homme est las d'écrire et la femme d'aimer.

Les maisons çà et là commençaient à fumer.
Les femmes de plaisir, la paupière livide,
Bouche ouverte, dormaient de leur sommeil stupide;
Les pauvresses, traînant leurs seins maigres et froids,
Soufflaient sur leurs tisons et soufflaient sur leurs doigts.

C'était l'heure où parmi le froid et la lésine
S'aggravent les douleurs des femmes en gésine;
Comme un sanglot coupé par un sang écumeux
Le chant du coq au loin déchirait l'air brumeux;
Une mer de brouillards baignait les édifices,
Et les agonisants dans le fond des hospices
Poussaient leur dernier râle en hoquets inégaux.
Les débauchés rentraient, brisés par leurs travaux.

L'aurore grelottante en robe rose et verte
S'avançait lentement sur la Seine déserte,
Et le sombre Paris, en se frottant les yeux,
Empoignait ses outils, vieillard laborieux.

Dawn of Day

Reveille rang out in the barracks square,
And street lights flickered in the morning air.

It was the time when dreams swarm, noxious,
And on their beds brown adolescents toss;
When, like a bleeding, throbbing, moving eye,
The lamplight makes a red stain on the day;
When, weighed down by the body rough, the soul
Like daylight with the light of lamps rebels.
A tearful face, its tears dried by the wind,
The atmosphere thrills with escaping things,
Man tires of writing, woman tires of love.

From chimneys here and there smoke curled above.
The harlots, with mascara round their eyes,
Slept open-mouthed, in silly sluggishness;
The beggar-women, dragging scraggy breasts,
Blew on their coals and hands, against the frost.

It was the time when, in the cold and shame,
Women in labour felt a sharper pain;
And, like a sob cut short by foaming blood,
The distant cockcrow rent the air bedewed;
A misty ocean bathed the capital,
And dying men remote in hospitals
In gasps unequal uttered their last sighs.
The rakes came home, broken by revelry.

Dawn, shivering in dress of pink and green,
Slowly advanced on the deserted Seine,
And sombre Paris, rubbing sleepy eyes,
Took up its tools, old man industrious.

Le Vin / Wine

L'Âme du vin

Un soir, l'âme du vin chantait dans les bouteilles:
«Homme, vers toi je pousse, ô cher déshérité,
Sous ma prison de verre et mes cires vermeilles,
Un chant plein de lumière et de fraternité!

«Je sais combien il faut, sur la colline en flamme,
De peine, de sueur et de soleil cuisant
Pour engendrer ma vie et pour me donner l'âme;
Mais je ne serai point ingrat ni malfaisant,

«Car j'éprouve une joie immense quand je tombe
Dans le gosier d'un homme usé par ses travaux,
Et sa chaude poitrine est une douce tombe
Où je me plais bien mieux que dans mes froids caveaux.

«Entends-tu retentir les refrains des dimanches
Et l'espoir qui gazouille en mon sein palpitant?
Les coudes sur la table et retroussant tes manches,
Tu me glorifieras et tu seras content;

«J'allumerai les yeux de ta femme ravie;
À ton fils je rendrai sa force et ses couleurs
Et serai pour ce frêle athlète de la vie
L'huile qui raffermit les muscles des lutteurs.

«En toi je tomberai, végétale ambroisie,
Grain précieux jeté par l'éternel Semeur,
Pour que de notre amour naisse la poésie
Qui jaillira vers Dieu comme une rare fleur!»

The Soul of the Wine

One evening, wine sang out with all its soul:
'I send you, Man, dear disinherited,
From my glass prison with its scarlet seals,
A song of sunshine and of brotherhood!

I know what toil upon the hill aflame,
What sweat and toil and scorching sun it needs
To give me life, give me a soul and name;
I shall not harm you, show ingratitude,

For I feel vast delight when I'm interred
In some deep-throated man, through toil grown old,
His warm breast is a grateful sepulchre
More pleasing, far, to me than cellars cold.

Hear you the echoing songs of holidays,
The hope which murmurs in my quivering breast?
Your sleeves rolled up, at table, at your ease,
You'll glorify me, with contentment blest;

I'll light the eyes of your delighted wife,
And to your son new strength and colour give,
And for this athlete delicate in life
I'll be the oil which makes the wrestler thrive.

I'll fall in you, ambrosia from the sky,
Rare seed by the eternal sower cast,
So that our love creates the poetry
Which like a flower shall praise the Holy Ghost!'

Fleurs du mal / Flowers of Evil

Épigraphe pour un livre condamné

Lecteur paisible et bucolique,
Sobre et naïf homme de bien,
Jette ce livre saturnien,
Orgiaque et mélancolique.

Si tu n'as fait ta rhétorique
Chez Satan, le rusé doyen,
Jette! tu n'y comprendrais rien,
Ou tu me croirais hystérique.

Mais si, sans se laisser charmer,
Ton œil sait plonger dans les gouffres,
Lis-moi, pour apprendre à m'aimer;

Âme curieuse qui souffres
Et vas cherchant ton paradis,
Plains-moi . . . Sinon je te maudis!

Epigraph for a Condemned Book

Reader domestic, tolerant,
Sober, unsullied, honest man,
Cast down this book Saturnian,
Voluptuous and virulent.

If rhetoric you have not learnt
From Satan's artful lexicon,
Cast it away, then, simpleton!
You'd think me worse than vehement.

But if, remaining free from spells,
Your eyes can plumb the hellish deep,
Read me, and learn to love me well;

O soul who wants to know, and weeps,
And goes in quest of paradise,
Have pity! . . . Or receive my curse!

La Destruction

Sans cesse à mes côtés s'agit le Démon;
Il nage autour de moi comme un air impalpable;
Je l'avale et le sens qui brûle mon poumon,
Et l'emplit d'un désir éternel et coupable.

Parfois il prend, sachant mon grand amour de l'Art,
La forme de la plus séduisante des femmes,
Et, sous de spécieux prétextes de cafard,
Accoutume ma lèvre à des philtres infâmes.

Il me conduit ainsi, loin du regard de Dieu,
Haletant et brisé de fatigue, au milieu
Des plaines de l'Ennui, profondes et désertes,

Et jette dans mes yeux pleins de confusion
Des vêtements souillés, des blessures ouvertes,
Et l'appareil sanglant de la Destruction!

Destruction

The Devil stirs beside me, constantly:
Floats round me like an air impalpable;
I feel him in my lungs, incendiary,
Bringing desires eternal, culpable.

Sometimes, aware of my great love of Art,
He takes a woman's shape, voluptuous,
And, with some lame excuse, the hypocrite,
Accustoms me to philtres infamous.

And so, far from God's sight, he leads me on,
Panting and broken with exhaustion,
Into the plains of Tedium profound,

And casts into my eyes confusion,
Worn, dirty clothes, open, infested wounds:
Deadly apparel of Destruction!

Femmes damnées

Comme un bétail pensif sur le sable couchées,
Elles tournent leurs yeux vers l'horizon des mers,
Et leurs pieds se cherchant et leurs mains rapprochées
Ont de douces langueurs et des frissons amers.

Les unes, cœurs épris de longues confidences,
Dans le fond des bosquets où jasent les ruisseaux,
Vont épelant l'amour des craintives enfances
Et creusent le bois vert des jeunes arbrisseaux;

D'autres, comme des sœurs, marchent lentes et graves
À travers les rochers pleins d'apparitions,
Où saint Antoine a vu surgir comme des laves
Les seins nus et pourprés de ses tentations;

Il en est, aux lueurs des résines croulantes,
Qui dans le creux muet des vieux antres païens
T'appellent au secours de leurs fièvres hurlantes,
Ô Bacchus, endormeur des remords anciens!

Et d'autres, dont la gorge aime les scapulaires,
Qui, recélant un fouet sous leurs longs vêtements,
Mêlent, dans le bois sombre et les nuits solitaires,
L'écume du plaisir aux larmes des tourments.

Ô vierges, ô démons, ô monstres, ô martyres,
De la réalité grands esprits contempteurs,
Chercheuses d'infini, dévotes et satyres,
Tantôt pleines de cris, tantôt pleines de pleurs,

Vous que dans votre enfer mon âme a poursuivies,
Pauvres sœurs, je vous aime autant que je vous plains,
Pour vos mornes douleurs, vos soifs inassouvies,
Et les urnes d'amour dont vos grands cœurs sont pleins!

Women Damned

Like ruminating cattle on the sands,
They turn their eyes towards the line of sea;
Their feet, which seek each other, and their hands,
Are sweet and languid, quiver bitterly.

Some of them, longing, loving to confide,
Deep in the groves where streams run chattering,
Spell out the love of childhoods terrified,
And delve into the green woods burgeoning.

Others, like sisters, grave and slow of pace,
Cross rocks peopled by apparitions;
St Anthony saw there, like lava, rise
The purple, bare breasts of temptations.

Some of them, in the light of torches wan,
In silent hollow caves, pagan retreats,
Ask you for help in their delirium,
O Bacchus, who can lull the old regrets!

And there are some whose breast loves scapulars,
Who hide a whip beneath their long attire,
And, lonely, under heavens with no stars,
Mingle the foam of joy with torment's tears.

O virgins, demons, monsters, martyrs all,
Great spirits scornful of reality,
Who seek the infinite, believers, trulls,
Enraptured, or in utter misery,

You whom my soul pursues into your hell,
Poor sisters, I both love and pity you,
For your sore griefs, your thirsts insatiable,
The love with which your great hearts overflow!

Révolte / Revolt

Les Litanies de Satan

Ô toi, le plus savant et le plus beau des Anges,
Dieu trahi par le sort et privé de louanges,

Ô Satan, prends pitié de ma longue misère!

Ô Prince de l'exil, à qui l'on a fait tort,
Et qui, vaincu, toujours te redresses plus fort,

Ô Satan, prends pitié de ma longue misère!

Toi qui sais tout, grand roi des choses souterraines,
Guérisseur familier des angoisses humaines,

Ô Satan, prends pitié de ma longue misère!

Toi qui, même aux lépreux, aux parias maudits,
Enseignes par l'amour le goût du Paradis,

Ô Satan, prends pitié de ma longue misère!

Ô toi qui de la Mort, ta vieille et forte amante,
Engendras l'Espérance – une folle charmante!

Ô Satan, prends pitié de ma longue misère!

Toi qui fais au proscrit ce regard calme et haut
Qui damne tout un peuple autour d'un échafaud,

Ô Satan, prends pitié de ma longue misère!

Toi qui sais en quels coins des terres envieuses
Le Dieu jaloux cacha les pierres précieuses,

Ô Satan, prends pitié de ma longue misère!

The Litanies of Satan

O thou, of Angels loveliest, most wise,
O God betrayed by fate, deprived of praise,

Satan, have mercy on my long distress!

O Prince of exile, who was dispossessed,
Who ever rises stronger when oppressed,

Satan, have mercy on my long distress!

O thou who knowest all, Hell's sovereign,
Known healer of mankind's afflictions,

Satan, have mercy on my long distress!

Thou who the lepers and pariahs doomed
Show out of love the Paradise to come,

Satan, have mercy on my long distress!

Thou who in Death, your mistress old and strong,
Breeds Hope – delightful aberration!

Satan, have mercy on my long distress!

Thou who dost give the outlaw the proud glance
Which damns the crowd who watch his sufferance,

Satan, have mercy on my long distress!

Thou who dost know where greedy earth enfolds
The precious stones a jealous God concealed,

Satan, have mercy on my long distress!

Toi dont l'œil clair connaît les profonds arsenaux
Où dort enseveli le peuple des métaux,

Ô Satan, prends pitié de ma longue misère!

Toi dont la large main cache les précipices
Au somnambule errant au bord des édifices,

Ô Satan, prends pitié de ma longue misère!

Toi qui, magiquement, assouplis les vieux os
De l'ivrogne attardé foulé par les chevaux,

Ô Satan, prends pitié de ma longue misère!

Toi qui, pour consoler l'homme frêle qui souffre,
Nous appris à mêler le salpêtre et le soufre,

Ô Satan, prends pitié de ma longue misère!

Toi qui poses ta marque, ô complice subtil,
Sur le front du Crésus impitoyable et vil,

Ô Satan, prends pitié de ma longue misère!

Toi qui mets dans les yeux et dans le cœur des filles
Le culte de la plaie et l'amour des guenilles,

Ô Satan, prends pitié de ma longue misère!

Bâton des exilés, lampe des inventeurs,
Confesseur des pendus et des conspirateurs,

Ô Satan, prends pitié de ma longue misère!

Père adoptif de ceux qu'en sa noire colère
Du paradis terrestre a chassés Dieu le Père,

Ô Satan, prends pitié de ma longue misère!

Thou whose clear eye knows the deep sepulchres
Where multitudes of metals lie interred,

Satan, have mercy on my long distress!

Thou whose great hand conceals the precipice
From the somnambulist whom roofs entice,

Satan, have mercy on my long distress!

Thou who by magic softens the old bones
Of loitering drunks by horses trampled down,

Satan, have mercy on my long distress!

Thou who, consoling frail mankind in pain,
Taught us to make our guns and gun-cotton,

Satan, have mercy on my long distress!

Thou who didst set thy mark, accomplice skilled,
Upon the heart of Crœsus harsh and vile,

Satan, have mercy on my long distress!

Thou who put into women's hearts and eyes
The cult of wounds, the love of poverty,

Satan, have mercy on my long distress!

Staff of the exile and discoverer,
Confessor of condemned conspirator,

Satan, have mercy on my long distress!

Father to those whom in his sombre wrath
God drove from his Paradise on earth,

Satan, have mercy on my long distress!

PRIÈRE

Gloire et louange à toi, Satan, dans les hauteurs
Du Ciel, où tu régnas, et dans les profondeurs
De l'Enfer, où, vaincu, tu rêves en silence!
Fais que mon âme un jour, sous l'Arbre de Science,
Près de toi se repose, à l'heure où sur ton front,
Comme un Temple nouveau ses rameaux s'épandront!

PRAYER

To thee, o Satan, glory be, and praise,
In Heaven, once thy kingdom, the abyss
Of Hell, where, now, thou dreamest silently!
Grant that my soul, one day, beneath the Tree
Of Knowledge, may rest near thee, when o'erhead,
Like a new Temple, its wide branches spread!

La Mort / Death

La Mort des amants

Nous aurons des lits pleins d'odeurs légères,
Des divans profonds comme des tombeaux,
Et d'étranges fleurs sur des étagères,
Écloses pour nous sous des cieux plus beaux.

Usant à l'envi leurs chaleurs dernières,
Nos deux cœurs seront deux vastes flambeaux,
Qui réfléchiront leurs doubles lumières
Dans nos deux esprits, ces miroirs jumeaux.

Un soir fait de rose et de bleu mystique,
Nous échangerons un éclair unique,
Comme un long sanglot, tout chargé d'adieux;

Et plus tard un Ange, entr'ouvrant les portes,
Viendra ranimer, fidèle et joyeux,
Les miroirs ternis et les flammes mortes.

The Death of Lovers

We shall have beds full of aromas light,
Divans profound and deep as sepulchres,
And shelves of flowers rare and exquisite
Which bloomed for us where skies are lovelier.

And when in their last warmth our hearts delight,
They will be like two torches without peer,
Which will reflect their splendour doubly bright
In our two spirits, which twin mirrors are.

One evening roseate, cerulean,
We shall exchange a single lightning gleam,
Like a long sob, all heavy with farewells;

And, later, Angels, opening the doors,
Will come, faithful and joyous sentinels,
And the dull mirrors and dead fires restore.

La Mort des pauvres

C'est la Mort qui console, hélas! et qui fait vivre;
C'est le but de la vie, et c'est le seul espoir
Qui, comme un élixir, nous monte et nous enivre,
Et nous donne le cœur de marcher jusqu'au soir;

À travers la tempête, et la neige, et le givre,
C'est la clarté vibrante à notre horizon noir;
C'est l'auberge fameuse inscrite sur le livre,
Où l'on pourra manger, et dormir, et s'asseoir;

C'est un Ange qui tient dans ses doigts magnétiques
Le sommeil et le don des rêves extatiques,
Et qui refait le lit des gens pauvres et nus;

C'est la gloire des Dieux, c'est le grenier mystique,
C'est la bourse du pauvre et sa patrie antique,
C'est le portique ouvert sur les Cieux inconnus!

The Death of the Poor

It is Death which consoles, alas! and makes us live;
It is the aim of life, the one aspiration
Which lifts us, elates us, draught restorative,
And gives us the heart to walk till day is done.

When the snow and frost lie thick, and tempests drive
In darkness, it is the light that leads us on;
It is the inn, they say, superlative,
Where we can eat and drink, sleep and sit down;

It is an Angel with authority
To give us sleep and our dreams of ecstasy,
An Angel who makes the bed of the naked poor.

It is the glory of Gods, and the mystic granary,
The purse of the poor, and their land eternally,
It is the gate to Heavens unknown before!

Le Voyage

À Maxime du Camp

i

Pour l'enfant, amoureux de cartes et d'estampes,
L'univers est égal à son vaste appétit.
Ah! que le monde est grand à la clarté des lampes!
Aux yeux du souvenir que le monde est petit!

Un matin nous partons, le cerveau plein de flamme,
Le cœur gros de rancune et de désirs amers,
Et nous allons, suivant le rythme de la lame,
Berçant notre infini sur le fini des mers:

Les uns, joyeux de fuir une patrie infâme;
D'autres, l'horreur de leurs berceaux, et quelques-uns,
Astrologues noyés dans les yeux d'une femme,
La Circé tyrannique aux dangereux parfums.

Pour n'être pas changés en bêtes, ils s'enivrent
D'espace et de lumière et de cieux embrasés;
La glace qui les mord, les soleils qui les cuivrent,
Effacent lentement la marque des baisers.

Mais les vrais voyageurs sont ceux-là seuls qui partent
Pour partir; cœurs légers, semblables aux ballons,
De leur fatalité jamais ils ne s'écartent,
Et, sans savoir pourquoi, disent toujours: Allons!

Ceux-là dont les désirs ont la forme des nues,
Et qui rêvent, ainsi qu'un conscrit de canon,
De vastes voluptés, changeantes, inconnues,
Et dont l'esprit humain n'a jamais su le nom!

The Voyage

To Maxime du Camp

i

The child in love with prints and gazetteers
Finds that the globe his thirst can satisfy.
How big the world by lamplight does appear!
How small the world is in our memory!

One morning we depart, the mind ablaze,
The heart weighed down with care and bitterness,
We go, according to the rhythmic seas,
Our vastness lull on ocean's littleness.

Some happily escape their country vile;
Others, the horror of their birth, and some,
Astrologers lost in a woman's smile,
The baneful Circe with her strong perfume.

So that she does not turn them into beasts,
They drink in burning skies and light and space;
The ice which bites, the suns which turn them rust,
Slowly efface the mark of her embrace.

But the real travellers are only those
Who leave for leaving's sake; hearts light as air,
They never do their destiny oppose;
Not knowing why, they always say: I dare!

They have desires immense and nebulous,
They dream, as conscripts of the cannon dream,
Of vast delights, changing, mysterious,
Of which mankind has never known the name!

ii

Nous imitons, horreur! la toupie et la boule
Dans leur valse et leurs bonds; même dans nos sommeils
La Curiosité nous tourmente et nous roule,
Comme un Ange cruel qui fouette des soleils.

Singulière fortune où le but se déplace,
Et, n'étant nulle part, peut être n'importe où!
Où l'Homme, dont jamais l'espérance n'est lasse,
Pour trouver le repos court toujours comme un fou!

Notre âme est un trois-mâts cherchant son Icarie;
Une voix retentit sur le pont: «Ouvre l'œil!»
Une voix de la hune, ardente et folle, crie:
«Amour ... gloire ... bonheur!» Enfer! c'est un écueil!

Chaque îlot signalé par l'homme de vigie
Est un Eldorado promis par le Destin;
L'Imagination qui dresse son orgie
Ne trouve qu'un récif aux clartés du matin.

Ô le pauvre amoureux des pays chimériques!
Faut-il le mettre aux fers, le jeter à la mer,
Ce matelot ivrogne, inventeur d'Amériques
Dont le mirage rend le gouffre plus amer?

Tel le vieux vagabond, piétinant dans la boue,
Rêve, le nez en l'air, de brillants paradis;
Son œil ensorcelé découvre une Capoue
Partout où la chandelle illumine un taudis.

iii

Étonnants voyageurs! quelles nobles histoires
Nous lisons dans vos yeux profonds comme les mers!
Montrez-nous les écrins de vos riches mémoires,
Ces bijoux merveilleux, faits d'astres et d'éthers.

ii

Alas! we're like the spinning-top and ball,
Waltzing and bounding; when our day is done
Still Curiosity, tyrannical,
Torments us: cruel Angel whipping suns.

Uncommon fortune where the goal can change,
And, being nowhere, can be anywhere!
Where Man, whose hope will never cease to range,
Runs always, madly, to seek rest elsewhere!

Our soul, three-master, seeks Icaria;
A voice cries from the bridge: 'Look out, all hands!'
One from the top, wild, cries: 'Utopia!
Love . . . glory . . . happiness!' It is quicksands.

Each islet signalled by the look-out man
Is Eldorado, and the gift of Fate;
Fancy, preparing celebration,
Finds only shallows in the morning light.

Poor lover of dreamlands and chimeras!
O must we chain him, cast him in the sea,
Drunk mariner who finds Americas
Whose mirage makes the gulf worse agony?

So some old vagabond tramples in mud,
And dreams, gazing aloft, of paradise;
Where'er the candle lights a hovel rude,
A Capua appears to his charmed eyes.

iii

Strange travellers! What noble histories
Lie hidden in your eyes deep as the seas!
Show us the caskets of your memories,
Those wondrous jewels made of galaxies.

Nous voulons voyager sans vapeur et sans voile!
Faites, pour égayer l'ennui de nos prisons,
Passer sur nos esprits, tendus comme une toile,
Vos souvenirs avec leurs cadres d'horizons.

Dites, qu'avez-vous vu?

iv

«Nous avons vu des astres
Et des flots; nous avons vu des sables aussi;
Et, malgré bien des chocs et d'imprévus désastres,
Nous nous sommes souvent ennuyés, comme ici.

«La gloire du soleil sur la mer violette,
La gloire des cités dans le soleil couchant,
Allumaient dans nos cœurs une ardeur inquiète
De plonger dans un ciel au reflet alléchant.

«Les plus riches cités, les plus grands paysages,
Jamais ne contenaient l'attrait mystérieux
De ceux que le hasard fait avec les nuages.
Et toujours le désir nous rendait soucieux!

«– La jouissance ajoute au désir de la force.
Désir, vieil arbre à qui le plaisir sert d'engrais,
Cependant que grossit et durcit ton écorce,
Tes branches veulent voir le soleil de plus près!

«Grandiras-tu toujours, grand arbre plus vivace
Que le cyprès? – Pourtant nous avons, avec soin,
Cueilli quelques croquis pour votre album vorace,
Frères qui trouvez beau tout ce qui vient de loin!

«Nous avons salué des idoles à trompe;
Des trônes constellés de joyaux lumineux;
Des palais ouvragés dont la féerique pompe
Serait pour vos banquiers un rêve ruineux;

We want to journey without steam or sail!
Liven our prison cells' monotony,
Pass through our spirits, stretched like canvas full,
Your recollections framed by sky and sea.

Tell us: what have you seen?

iv

                  'We have seen moon
And star; we have seen ocean and sea-shore;
Known many shocks, disasters unforeseen,
And we were often bored, as you are here.

The sun resplendent on the purple sea,
Cities resplendent in the setting sun,
Lit in our hearts a wild anxiety
To plunge in heaven's sweet reflection.

The richest cities, grandest scenery
Never contained the charm mysterious
Of those which clouds created in the sky.
And longing always made us anxious!

Enjoyment gives new vigour to desire.
Old tree which thrives on satisfaction,
Your bark hardens and grows with every year,
Your branches want to climb nearer the sun!

Will you still grow, tree more tenacious
Than cypress? – Nonetheless we've carefully
Brought sketches home, brothers voracious
Who love all things that come from overseas!

Idols with trunks we bowed before, and thrones
All starred with rubies, diamonds luminous;
Wrought palaces whose ostentation
Would for your bankers here be ruinous;

«Des costumes qui sont pour les yeux une ivresse;
Des femmes dont les dents et les ongles sont teints,
Et des jongleurs savants que le serpent caresse.»

v

Et puis, et puis encore?

vi

«Ô cerveaux enfantins!

Pour ne pas oublier la chose capitale,
Nous avons vu partout, et sans l'avoir cherché,
Du haut jusques en bas de l'échelle fatale,
Le spectacle ennuyeux de l'immortel péché:

«La femme, esclave vile, orgueilleuse et stupide,
Sans rire s'adorant et s'aimant sans dégoût;
L'homme, tyran goulu, paillard, dur et cupide,
Esclave de l'esclave et ruisseau dans l'égout;

«Le bourreau qui jouit, le martyr qui sanglote;
La fête qu'assaisonne et parfume le sang;
Le poison du pouvoir énervant le despote,
Et le peuple amoureux du fouet abrutissant;

«Plusieurs religions semblables à la nôtre,
Toutes escaladant le ciel; la Sainteté,
Comme en un lit de plume un délicat se vautre,
Dans les clous et le crin cherchant la volupté;

«L'Humanité bavarde, ivre de son génie,
Et, folle maintenant comme elle était jadis,
Criant à Dieu, dans sa furibonde agonie:
Ô mon semblable, ô mon maître, je te maudis!

Costumes which are elixir for the eyes;
Women with tinted teeth and tinted nails,
And skilful jugglers whom the snakes caress.'

v

And then, and then?

vi

           'O spirits infantile!

We don't forget the most important things,
We have seen everywhere, and seen unsought,
The wretched pageant of immortal sin,
From top to bottom of the steps of Fate:

Woman, slave idiotic, abject, proud,
Loving herself, unsmiling, unashamed,
Man, greedy tyrant, covetous and lewd,
Slave of the slave and in the sewer stream;

The happy torturer, martyr who weeps,
The festival seasoned and sweet with blood;
Poisonous power making despots weak,
And people amorous of being subdued.

A number of religions like our own,
All going heavenwards; and Holiness,
As someone dainty lolls in eiderdowns,
Seeking the nails and horse-hair that caress;

Prating mankind, drunk with its genius,
And mad today as it once used to be
Crying to God, in anguish furious,
"My equal, o my father, I curse thee!"

«Et les moins sots, hardis amants de la Démence,
Fuyant le grand troupeau parqué par le Destin,
Et se réfugiant dans l'opium immense!
– Tel est du globe entier l'éternel bulletin.»

vii

Amer savoir, celui qu'on tire du voyage!
Le monde, monotone et petit, aujourd'hui,
Hier, demain, toujours, nous fait voir notre image:
Une oasis d'horreur dans un désert d'ennui!

Faut-il partir? rester? Si tu peux rester, reste;
Pars, s'il le faut. L'un court, et l'autre se tapit
Pour tromper l'ennemi vigilant et funeste,
Le Temps! Il est, hélas! des coureurs sans répit,

Comme le Juif errant et comme les apôtres,
À qui rien ne suffit, ni wagon ni vaisseau,
Pour fuir ce rétiaire infâme; il en est d'autres
Qui savent le tuer sans quitter leur berceau.

Lorsque enfin il mettra le pied sur notre échine,
Nous pourrons espérer et crier: En avant!
De même qu'autrefois nous partions pour la Chine,
Les yeux fixés au large et les cheveux au vent,

Nous nous embarquerons sur la mer des Ténèbres
Avec le cœur joyeux d'un jeune passager.
Entendez-vous ces voix, charmantes et funèbres,
Qui chantent: «Par ici! vous qui voulez manger

«Le Lotus parfumé! c'est ici qu'on vendange
Les fruits miraculeux dont votre cœur a faim;
Venez vous enivrer de la douceur étrange
De cette après-midi qui n'a jamais de fin!»

And the least dim, who love Delirium,
Escaping the great flock which Fate enfolds,
And taking refuge in vast opium!
– That ever is the way of all the world!'

vii

What bitter wisdom does the voyage give!
The world, small, dull, today and yesterday,
Tomorrow, will our likeness still revive:
Oasis grim in our Sahara grey!

Must we depart or stay? Stay, if you can;
Leave, if you must. Some run, and others squat
To cheat Time: ever watchful and malign.
And some there are who run without respite,

Like the apostles and the Wandering Jew,
Nothing suffices them, coach, brigantine,
To flee this gladiator foul; then, too,
Others can kill him while they're still unweaned.

And when he treads us down, on the last day,
We shall still hope and cry: Forward! Go on!
Just as we once set out for far Cathay,
Blown by the wind, watching the ocean,

We shall embark upon the sea of Gloom
Like a young passenger, with joyful heart.
Hear you these voices charming, full of doom,
Which sing: 'Come hither, you who want to eat

The fragrant Lotus! It is here you cull
The fruits miraculous your heart adores;
Grow drunk with the delights ineffable
Of afternoons which last for evermore!'

À l'accent familier nous devinons le spectre;
Nos Pylades là-bas tendent leurs bras vers nous.
«Pour rafraîchir ton cœur nage vers ton Électre!»
Dit celle dont jadis nous baisions les genoux.

viii

Ô Mort, vieux capitaine, il est temps! levons l'ancre.
Ce pays nous ennuie, ô Mort! Appareillons!
Si le ciel et la mer sont noirs comme de l'encre,
Nos cœurs que tu connais sont remplis de rayons!

Verse-nous ton poison pour qu'il nous réconforte!
Nous voulons, tant ce feu nous brûle le cerveau,
Plonger au fond du gouffre, Enfer ou Ciel, qu'importe?
Au fond de l'Inconnu pour trouver du *nouveau*!

We guess the ghost from the familiar tone;
Our Pylades stretch out their arms to us.
'Refresh your heart! To your Electra come!'
Says she whose knees we once kissed, tremulous.

viii

O Death, old captain, it is time! Set sail!
This land palls on us, Death! Let's put to sea!
If sky and ocean are black as coal,
You know our hearts are full of brilliancy!

Pour forth your poison, our deliverance!
This fire consumes our minds, let's bid adieu,
Plumb Hell or Heaven, what's the difference?
Plumb the Unknown, to find out something *new*!

LES ÉPAVES / THE WRECKAGE

Pièces condamnées / Condemned Poems

Femmes damnées

DELPHINE ET HIPPOLYTE

À la pâle clarté des lampes languissantes,
Sur de profonds coussins tout imprégnés d'odeur,
Hippolyte rêvait aux caresses puissantes
Qui levaient le rideau de sa jeune candeur.

Elle cherchait, d'un œil troublé par la tempête,
De sa naïveté le ciel déjà lointain,
Ainsi qu'un voyageur qui retourne la tête
Vers les horizons bleus dépassés le matin.

De ses yeux amortis les paresseuses larmes,
L'air brisé, la stupeur, la morne volupté,
Ses bras vaincus, jetés comme de vaines armes,
Tout servait, tout parait sa fragile beauté.

Étendue à ses pieds, calme et pleine de joie,
Delphine la couvait avec des yeux ardents
Comme un animal fort qui surveille une proie
Après l'avoir d'abord marquée avec les dents.

Beauté forte à genoux devant la beauté frêle,
Superbe, elle humait voluptueusement
Le vin de son triomphe, et s'allongeait vers elle,
Comme pour recueillir un doux remercîment.

Elle cherchait dans l'œil de sa pâle victime,
Le cantique muet que chante le plaisir,
Et cette gratitude infinie et sublime
Qui sort de la paupière ainsi qu'un long soupir.

– «Hippolyte, cher cœur, que dis-tu de ces choses?
Comprends-tu maintenant qu'il ne faut pas offrir
L'holocauste sacré de tes premières roses
Aux souffles violents qui pourraient les flétrir?

Women Damned

DELPHINE AND HIPPOLYTA

Lit palely by the lustres languishing,
On cushions deep with perfume redolent,
Hippolyta recalled caresses sovereign
Which had unveiled her youthful innocence.

She sought, with eyes still troubled by the storm,
The sky of purity, now far away,
Like a departing traveller who turns
To see the landscape he passed yesterday.

The lazy tears that fell from her dulled eyes,
The broken air, the stupor, the delight,
Her vanquished arms, cast down in armistice,
All served, adorned her beauty delicate.

Reclining at her feet, calm, full of joy,
Delphine devoured her with her ardent eyes
As a strong animal observes its prey
When with its teeth it has marked out the prize.

Strong beauty kneeling to the beauty frail,
Superb, she savoured in an ecstasy
The wine of triumph, and came closer still
As if she did sweet thankfulness foresee.

She gazed intently at her victim pale,
And sought the silent hymn that pleasure sings,
The gratitude endless and magical
Which eyes express, a wordless offering.

– 'Hippolyta, what now, my precious one?
Do you now understand you must not make
The sacred sacrifice of your first rose
To violent storms which might its petals take?

«Mes baisers sont légers comme ces éphémères
Qui caressent le soir les grands lacs transparents,
Et ceux de ton amant creuseront leurs ornières
Comme des chariots ou des socs déchirants;

«Ils passeront sur toi comme un lourd attelage
De chevaux et de bœufs aux sabots sans pitié ...
Hippolyte, ô ma sœur! tourne donc ton visage,
Toi, mon âme et mon cœur, mon tout et ma moitié,

«Tourne vers moi tes yeux pleins d'azur et d'étoiles!
Pour un de ces regards charmants, baume divin,
Des plaisirs plus obscurs je lèverai les voiles
Et je t'endormirai dans un rêve sans fin!»

Mais Hippolyte alors, levant sa jeune tête:
– «Je ne suis point ingrate et ne me repens pas,
Ma Delphine, je souffre et je suis inquiète,
Comme après un nocturne et terrible repas.

«Je sens fondre sur moi de lourdes épouvantes
Et de noirs bataillons de fantômes épars,
Qui veulent me conduire en des routes mouvantes
Qu'un horizon sanglant ferme de toutes parts.

«Avons-nous donc commis une action étrange?
Explique, si tu peux, mon trouble et mon effroi;
Je frissonne de peur quand tu me dis: «Mon ange!»
Et cependant je sens ma bouche aller vers toi.

«Ne me regarde pas ainsi, toi, ma pensée!
Toi que j'aime à jamais, ma sœur d'élection,
Quand même tu serais une embûche dressée
Et le commencement de ma perdition!»

Delphine secouant sa crinière tragique,
Et comme trépignant sur le trépied de fer,

My kisses are as gentle as day-flies
At eventide, embracing lakes serene,
And those of men their ruts will multiply
Like chariots or ploughshares harrowing.

They will pass over you, a heavy team
Of oxen, with their hooves unmerciful . . .
Hippolyta: look at me, dearest one,
O you my soul and heart, my half and all,

Show me your eyes full of blue skies and stars!
For one enchanting look, a balm divine,
I'll lift the veil from pleasures more obscure,
And make you sleep on in an endless dream!'

But then Hippolyta raised her young head:
– 'I am not thankless, I do not repent,
My Delphine, I am anxious, afraid,
As after nights in dreadful feasting spent.

I feel some heavy terror fall on me,
And black battalions of spectres thin,
Who want to lead me along moving ways
On every side by ruthless skies shut in.

Have we then done a deed remarkable?
Can you explain my trouble and my fear?
I tremble when you say to me: "My jewel!"
And yet I search, and hope your lips are near.

O look not on me so, my own delight!
You whom I ever love, sister I choose,
Even if you should be the ambush set,
The love for whom salvation I lose!'

Then Delphine, like a tragic prophetess
Upon the tripod, shook her mane of hair,

L'œil fatal, répondit d'une voix despotique:
– «Qui donc devant l'amour ose parler d'enfer?

«Maudit soit à jamais le rêveur inutile
Qui voulut le premier, dans sa stupidité,
S'éprenant d'un problème insoluble et stérile,
Aux choses de l'amour mêler l'honnêteté!

«Celui qui veut unir dans un accord mystique
L'ombre avec la chaleur, la nuit avec le jour,
Ne chauffera jamais son corps paralytique
À ce rouge soleil que l'on nomme l'amour!

«Va, si tu veux, chercher un fiancé stupide;
Cours offrir un cœur vierge à ses cruels baisers;
Et, pleine de remords et d'horreur, et livide,
Tu me rapporteras tes seins stigmatisés . . .

«On ne peut ici bas contenter qu'un seul maître!»
Mais l'enfant, épanchant une immense douleur,
Cria soudain: – «Je sens élargir dans mon être
Un abîme béant; cet abîme est mon cœur!

«Brûlant comme un volcan, profond comme le vide!
Rien ne rassasiera ce monstre gémissant
Et ne rafraîchira la soif de l'Euménide
Qui, la torche à la main, le brûle jusqu'au sang.

«Que nos rideaux fermés nous séparent du monde,
Et que la lassitude amène le repos!
Je veux m'anéantir dans ta gorge profonde,
Et trouver sur ton sein la fraîcheur des tombeaux!»

– Descendez, descendez, lamentables victimes,
Descendez le chemin de l'enfer éternel!
Plongez au plus profond du gouffre, où tous les crimes,
Flagellés par un vent qui ne vient pas du ciel,

And, fatal-eyed, replied with despot's voice:
'Who, knowing love, to speak of hell would dare?

Cursed be the dreamer ineffectual
Who first desired, in his stupidity,
Loving a problem void, insoluble,
To mingle thoughts of love with honesty!

He who would join in mystic harmony
Summer and winter, morning light and eve,
Will not his useless body gratify
In this red sunshine which is known as love!

Go, if you will, and seek some stupid swain;
Run, give a virgin heart to his harsh kiss;
And full of horror and remorse and pain,
You will bring back to me your branded breasts ...

You can serve but one master here below!'
But now the girl her vast grief did impart,
Cried suddenly: 'O in my soul there grows
A yawning void – and this void is my heart!

Ablaze, volcanic, deep as emptiness!
Nothing will satisfy this groaning beast
Or quench the thirst of the Eumenides
Who, torch in hand, burns deep into its flesh!

Let our drawn curtains keep us from the world,
And may my weariness bring me repose!
May I in your deep bosom be annulled,
Find on your breast a cool necropolis!'

– Go down, go down, o victims pitiful,
Go down the path of everlasting doom,
Where all crimes are consumed in deepest hell,
Scourged by a wind which not from heaven comes,

Bouillonnent pêle-mêle avec un bruit d'orage.
Ombres folles, courez au but de vos désirs;
Jamais vous ne pourrez assouvir votre rage,
Et votre châtiment naîtra de vos plaisirs.

Jamais un rayon frais n'éclaira vos cavernes;
Par les fentes des murs des miasmes fiévreux
Filtrent en s'enflammant ainsi que des lanternes
Et pénètrent vos corps de leurs parfums affreux.

L'âpre stérilité de votre jouissance
Altère votre soif et roidit votre peau,
Et le vent furibond de la concupiscence
Fait claquer votre chair ainsi qu'un vieux drapeau.

Loin des peuples vivants, errantes, condamnées,
À travers les déserts courez comme des loups;
Faites votre destin, âmes désordonnées,
Et fuyez l'infini que vous portez en vous!

And boil in ferment like a raging storm.
Wild shades, run to the end of your desires;
Never will you assuage your passion,
Your pleasures will your punishment inspire.

Never did sunlight in your caverns shine;
Through crannies in the wall miasms foul
Seep and, like lanterns, kindle into flame,
And poison you with their mephitic smell.

The bitter barrenness of your delight
Makes you more thirsty, and dries up your skin,
The raging tempest of your appetite
Makes your flesh flap: a banner long since gone.

Far from the world, condemned and vagabond,
Run like the wolves beneath Sahara skies,
Pursue your destiny, spirits deranged,
Flee the infinity that in you lies!

Le Léthé

Viens sur mon cœur, âme cruelle et sourde,
Tigre adoré, monstre aux airs indolents;
Je veux longtemps plonger mes doigts tremblants
Dans l'épaisseur de ta crinière lourde;

Dans tes jupons remplis de ton parfum
Ensevelir ma tête endolorie,
Et respirer, comme une fleur flétrie,
Le doux relent de mon amour défunt.

Je veux dormir! dormir plutôt que vivre!
Dans un sommeil aussi doux que la mort,
J'étalerai mes baisers sans remord
Sur ton beau corps poli comme le cuivre.

Pour engloutir mes sanglots apaisés
Rien ne vaut l'abîme de ta couche;
L'oubli puissant habite sur ta bouche,
Et le Léthé coule dans tes baisers.

À mon destin, désormais mon délice,
J'obéirai comme un prédestiné;
Martyr docile, innocent condamné,
Dont la ferveur attise le supplice,

Je sucerai, pour noyer ma rancœur,
Le népenthès et la bonne ciguë
Aux bouts charmants de cette gorge aiguë
Qui n'a jamais emprisonné de cœur.

Lethe

Come to my breast, soul hard and passionless,
Beloved tiger, beast with languid airs;
I want to plunge my hands into your hair
Heavy and thick, in tremulous caress;

In petticoats all fragrant with your scent
Bury my aching and uneasy head,
And breathe in, like a flower long since dead,
The musty sweetness of my love now spent.

I want to sleep – to sleep rather than live!
In sleep as gentle as eternity,
I shall spread out my kisses ruthlessly
Upon your copper skin superlative.

I know of nowhere like your bed's abyss
To swallow up my agony, now gone;
Upon your lips dwells great oblivion,
And Lethe flows on in your every kiss.

My destiny is henceforth my delight,
And like a destined man I shall consent;
A docile martyr, victim innocent,
Whose very fervour makes the flames burn bright.

And I shall drink, to drown my bitterness,
Nepenthe and refreshing hellebore
From those sharp-pointed breasts that I adore,
Which never held a heart under duress.

À celle qui est trop gaie

Ta tête, ton geste, ton air
Sont beaux comme un beau paysage;
Le rire joue en ton visage
Comme un vent frais dans un ciel clair.

Le passant chagrin que tu frôles
Est ébloui par la santé
Qui jaillit comme une clarté
De tes bras et de tes épaules.

Les retentissantes couleurs
Dont tu parsèmes tes toilettes
Jettent dans l'esprit des poëtes
L'image d'un ballet de fleurs.

Ces robes folles sont l'emblème
De ton esprit bariolé;
Folle dont je suis affolé,
Je te hais autant que je t'aime!

Quelquefois dans un beau jardin
Où je traînais mon atonie,
J'ai senti, comme une ironie,
Le soleil déchirer mon sein;

Et le printemps et la verdure
Ont tant humilié mon cœur,
Que j'ai puni sur une fleur
L'insolence de la Nature.

Ainsi je voudrais, une nuit,
Quand l'heure de la volupté sonne,
Vers les trésors de ta personne,
Comme un lâche, ramper sans bruit,

To One Who Is Too Gay

Your head, your gesture and your air
Are like a landscape beautiful;
And on your face there plays a smile:
A fresh wind in a heaven clear.

The gloomy stranger whom you pass
Is dazzled by the health and bloom
Which flashes like the light of noon
From arms and shoulders bounteous.

The colours loud and clamorous
With which you deck out every dress
Upon the poet's mind impress
The image of a dance of flowers.

The clothes extravagant you wear
Reflect your multicoloured mind;
I'm mad on you, mad womankind,
I hate you as I hold you dear!

At moments, in some garden fair
Where I dragged on my atony,
I felt, relentless irony,
The sunlight at my bosom tear;

And spring and green luxuriance
Did so humiliate my heart
That I would pull a flower apart
To punish Nature's insolence.

And so, beneath a sombre sky,
When comes the moment for delight,
I'll seek the treasure of your night,
Creep like a coward, noiselessly,

Pour châtier ta chair joyeuse,
Pour meurtrir ton sein pardonné,
Et faire à ton flanc étonné
Une blessure large et creuse,

Et, vertigineuse douceur!
À travers ces lèvres nouvelles,
Plus éclatantes et plus belles,
T'infuser mon vénin, ma sœur!

Chastise your body jubilant,
And bruise your now-forgiven breast,
Inflict upon your side aghast
A wound hollow and insolent,

And, paradise beyond compare,
Through these new lips equivocal,
More brilliant, more beautiful,
Infuse my spleen in you, my dear!

Les Bijoux

La très-chère était nue, et, connaissant mon cœur,
Elle n'avait gardé que ses bijoux sonores,
Dont le riche attirail lui donnait l'air vainqueur
Qu'ont dans leurs jours heureux les esclaves des Mores.

Quand il jette en dansant son bruit vif et moqueur,
Ce monde rayonnant de métal et de pierre
Me ravit en extase, et j'aime à la fureur
Les choses où le son se mêle à la lumière.

Elle était donc couchée et se laissait aimer,
Et du haut du divan elle souriait d'aise
À mon amour profond et doux comme la mer,
Qui vers elle montait comme vers sa falaise.

Les yeux fixés sur moi, comme un tigre dompté,
D'un air vague et rêveur elle essayait des poses,
Et la candeur unie à la lubricité
Donnait un charme neuf à ses métamorphoses;

Et son bras et sa jambe, et sa cuisse et ses reins,
Polis comme de l'huile, onduleux comme un cygne,
Passaient devant mes yeux clairvoyants et sereins;
Et son ventre et ses seins, ces grappes de ma vigne,

S'avançaient, plus câlins que le Anges du mal,
Pour troubler le repos où mon âme était mise,
Et pour la déranger du rocher de cristal
Où, calme et solitaire, elle s'était assise.

Je croyais voir unis par un nouveau dessin
Les hanches de l'Antiope au buste d'un imberbe,
Tant sa taille faisait ressortir son bassin.
Sur ce teint fauve et brun le fard était superbe!

The Jewels

My love was naked; since she knew my prayer,
She wore only her jewels sonorous,
Whose rich abundance gave her the proud air
Of Moorish slaves in days victorious.

It dances, ringing sharp in mockery,
This shining world of metal and of stone:
Enraptures me, I love with ecstasy
The things where sound and brilliance are one.

So she reclined, and let herself be loved,
And from the high divan with pleasure smiled
Upon my love deep, gentle as the waves,
Which rose towards her, promontory wild.

She watched me, lion in captivity,
Reflective, dreamy, she tried every pose,
Her artlessness and her lubricity
Gave new charm to each metamorphosis;

Her arms and legs, her buttocks and her loins,
Gleaming like oil and gliding like a swan,
She showed my eyes clearsighted and serene;
Her belly, and her breasts, grapes of my vine,

Came near, more tempting than the Prince of Hell,
To break the peace which did enfold my heart,
And move it from the crystal citadel
Where it had rested, peaceful and apart.

I seemed to see joined in a new design
The torso of a boy, Diana's thighs,
So did her hips her slim waist underline.
She rouged her brown cheeks – splendid artifice!

– Et la lampe s'étant résignée à mourir,
Comme le foyer seul illuminait la chambre,
Chaque fois qu'il poussait un flamboyant soupir,
Il inondait de sang cette peau couleur d'ambre!

– And since the lamp resigned itself to die,
And now the fire alone lit up the room,
Each time it uttered a flamboyant sigh,
It flushed with blood her amber-coloured skin!

Galanteries / Gallantries

Les Yeux de Berthe

Vous pouvez mépriser les yeux les plus célèbres,
Beaux yeux de mon enfant, par où filtre et s'enfuit
Je ne sais quoi de bon, de doux comme la Nuit!
Beaux yeux, versez sur moi vos charmantes ténèbres!

Grands yeux de mon enfant, arcanes adorés,
Vous ressemblez beaucoup à ces grottes magiques
Où, derrière l'amas des ombres léthargiques,
Scintillent vaguement des trésors ignorés!

Mon enfant a des yeux obscurs, profonds et vastes,
Comme toi, Nuit immense, éclairés comme toi!
Leurs feux sont ces pensers d'Amour, mêlés de Foi,
Qui pétillent au fond, voluptueux ou chastes.

Bertha's Eyes

You can despise the most illustrious eyes,
Fine eyes of my dear love, through which there flows
Something as good and kind as Night bestows!
Fine eyes, give me your shadows rapturous!

Great eyes of my dear love, nostrums adored,
You're very like those old enchanted caves
In which, beyond dull shadows, one perceives
The vague gleam of an unknown treasure-hoard!

My love has eyes obscure, profound and vast,
Like you, lit up like you, great Night above!
Their fires are thoughts of Faith, mingled with Love,
Which sparkle in the depths, profane or chaste.

Hymne

À la très-chère, à la très-belle
Qui remplit mon cœur de clarté,
À l'ange, à l'idole immortelle,
Salut en l'immortalité!

Elle se répand dans ma vie
Comme un air imprégné de sel,
Et dans mon âme inassouvie
Verse le goût de l'éternel.

Sachet toujours frais qui parfume
L'atmosphère d'un cher réduit,
Encensoir oublié qui fume
En secret à travers la nuit,

Comment, amour incorruptible,
T'exprimer avec vérité?
Grain de musc qui gis, invisible,
Au fond de mon éternité!

À la très-bonne, à la très-belle
Qui fait ma joie et ma santé,
À l'ange, à l'idole immortelle,
Salut en l'immortalité!

Hymn

To the most lovely, the most dear,
Who fills my heart with clarity,
The angel, idol I adore,
All hail in immortality!

She suffuses all my days,
Like a salt wind blowing free,
And does my hungry soul allay
With foretaste of eternity.

O perfume ever fresh which fills
The air of my beloved retreat,
Forgotten censer, fragrant still,
Fragrant in secret through the night,

How can I, faultless love, define
Your nature, tell it truthfully?
O speck of musk that lies, unseen,
Deep down in my eternity!

To the most lovely and the best,
Who is both health and joy to me,
The angel, goddess manifest,
All hail in immortality!

Les Promesses d'un visage

J'aime, ô pâle beauté, tes sourcils surbaissés,
  D'où semblent couler des ténèbres;
Tes yeux, quoique très-noirs, m'inspirent des pensers
  Qui ne sont pas du tout funèbres.

Tes yeux, qui sont d'accord avec tes noirs cheveux,
  Avec ta crinière élastique,
Tes yeux, languissament, me disent: «Si tu veux,
  Amant de la muse plastique,

«Suivre l'espoir qu'en toi nous avons excité,
  Et tous les goûts que tu professes,
Tu pourras constater notre véracité
  Depuis le nombril jusqu'aux fesses;

«Tu trouveras au bout de deux beaux seins bien lourds,
  Deux larges médailles de bronze,
Et sous un ventre uni, doux comme du velours,
  Bistré comme la peau d'un bonze,

«Une riche toison qui, vraiment, est la sœur
  De cette énorme chevelure,
Souple et frisée, et qui t'égale en épaisseur,
  Nuit sans étoiles, Nuit obscur!»

The Promises of a Face

I love, pale beauty, your elliptic brows,
   Whence shadows seem to flow;
Your eyes, though raven-black, do not impose
   Dejection or woe.

Your eyes, in harmony with your black hair,
   Your dark and buoyant mane,
Your eyes, languidly, tell me: 'If you care,
   Since art is your domain,

To realize the hopes that you possess,
   The tastes you advertise,
Then you may verify our truthfulness
   From the navel to the thighs.

You'll find two splendid breasts, heavy and full,
   Tipped by large discs of bronze,
And under a smooth belly, silken-cool
   And tawny like a Bonze,

A fleece luxuriant: the sister true
   Of this vast head of hair,
Compliant, curly, and as thick as you,
   Dark night, and starless air!'

Pièces diverses / Miscellaneous Poems

La Rançon

L'homme a, pour payer sa rançon,
Deux champs au tuf profond et riche,
Qu'il faut qu'il remue et défriche
Avec le fer de la raison;

Pour obtenir la moindre rose,
Pour extorquer quelques épis,
Des pleurs salés de son front gris
Sans cesse il faut qu'il les arrose.

L'un est l'Art, et l'autre l'Amour.
— Pour rendre le juge propice
Lorsque de la stricte justice
Paraîtra le terrible jour,

Il faudra lui montrer des granges
Pleines de moissons, et des fleurs
Dont les formes et les couleurs
Gagnent le suffrage des Anges.

The Ransom

To pay his ransom, man can claim
Two fields with tufa rich, profound,
Which with the iron of his mind
He has to turn up and reclaim;

If he the smallest rose would grow,
Extort an ear or two of corn,
He has to water them till doom
With the salt tears of his grey brow.

One field is Art, the other Love.
– To make the judge benevolent,
When, dreadful, strict, omnipotent,
The day of judgment dawns above,

He'll have to show him his full barns
Of wheat and corn, and show him flowers
Whose forms and colours do empower
The Angels to be partisan.

À une Malabaraise

Tes pieds sont aussi fins que tes mains, et ta hanche
Est large à faire envie à la plus belle blanche;
À l'artiste pensif ton corps est doux et cher;
Tes grands yeux de velours sont plus noirs que ta chair.
Aux pays chauds et bleus où ton dieu t'a fait naître,
Ta tâche est d'allumer la pipe de ton maître,
De pourvoir les flacons d'eaux fraîches et d'odeurs,
De chasser loin du lit les moustiques rôdeurs,
Et, dès que le matin fait chanter les platanes,
D'acheter au bazar ananas et bananes.
Tout le jour, où tu veux, tu mènes tes pieds nus,
Et fredonnes tout bas de vieux airs inconnus;
Et quand descend le soir au manteau d'écarlate,
Tu poses doucement ton corps sur une natte,
Où tes rêves flottants sont pleins de colibris,
Et toujours, comme toi, gracieux et fleuris.

Pourquoi, l'heureuse enfant, veux-tu voir notre France,
Ce pays trop peuplé que fauche la souffrance,
Et, confiant ta vie aux bras forts des marins
Faire de grands adieux à tes chers tamarins?
Toi, vêtue à moitié de mousselines frêles,
Frissonnante là-bas sous la neige et les grêles,
Comme tu pleurerais tes loisirs doux et francs,
Si, le corset brutal emprisonnant tes flancs,
Il te fallait glaner ton souper dans nos fanges
Et vendre le parfum de tes charmes étranges,
L'œil pensif, et suivant, dans nos sales brouillards,
Des cocotiers absents les fantômes épars!

1840

To a Girl in Malabar

Your feet are slender like your hands, your hips
Would those of any body white eclipse;
The pensive artist finds you benison;
Your velvet eyes are blacker than your skin.
In blue and sultry lands where you saw day,
You have to light your master's pipe alway,
The flasks with waters fresh and scents provide,
And chase roaming mosquitoes from the bed,
And when the plane trees sing, matutinal,
Buy pineapples, bananas from the stall.
All day you take your bare feet where you will,
Hum old forgotten tunes, scarce audible;
And, when the sun's red cloak falls in the west,
Upon a rush mat, quietly, you rest,
Where floating dreams are all of humming birds,
And all, like you, graceful and decked with flowers.

Why, happy child, do you need to see France,
This crowded land laid low by sufferance,
Entrust your life to strong-armed mariners,
Bid farewell to your tamarinds so dear?
You, half-clad in your gauze and muslin frail,
Would shiver here beneath the snow and hail,
And how you'd mourn your sweet and honest ease,
If, kept by brutal corsets in duress,
You gleaned your supper from our wickedness,
And sold your fragrant charms mysterious:
Pursued, through our dense fogs, with thoughtful eyes,
Thin ghosts of coco-palms on promontories!

INDEX OF TITLES

INDEX OF FIRST LINES